Sunday School 87/88 3.95
Grade ⑤/6.
Leslie Alber...

LESLIE ALBERDA

The mystery of Old Abe

W. G. Vandehulst

The mystery of Old Abe

PAIDEIA PRESS
St. Catharines, Ontario, Canada

First published in Dutch as *Ouwe Bram*, © G.F. Callen-
bach B. V. of Nijkerk. Translated by Harry der
Nederlanden.

ISBN 0-88815-755-X
Printed in the United States of America.

Table of Contents

1. Nosy Boys

It was dusk on a stormy spring evening. On the narrow dike along the floodlands where the reeds grow tall, three boys struggled bravely against the wild wind.

They tugged their hats down low on their foreheads, and pushed their hands deep into their pockets.

The wind tore at them with fierce gusts. It plastered their pants tightly against their knees, billowed their shirts out behind them, and howled into their glowing faces. But their eyes sparkled at the wind's challenge and they strode on bravely, leaning into every gust.

"Look there! Say, shall we . . . ?"

"What?" panted Jimmy, the youngest and the smallest of the three. Sometimes he would fall back a few paces, but every time he put on a little burst of speed and caught up with his friends again. "What's up?"

"Yeah! Neat!" cried Hugh. "Old Abe's cabin!" The husky boy who spoke is actually named Hugo, but people always call him Hugh.

"Where?" asked Jimmy, a hint of worry in his voice.

"Over there! And he's home, too. There's a light on!"

"Oh!" said Jimmy relieved. "I thought . . . ."

"You thought that the old man was already behind you with his stick, didn't you?" laughed Henry Hoover. He had been the first one to spot the distant glimmer of light through the bushes.

"Would you like to hide behind me, Jimmy?" teased Hugh. "Are you afraid Old Abe will see you?" Jimmy mumbled some reply, but the wind blew his words away.

"Say!" said Henry, whispering. "Shall we go and bang on Old Abe's door? Or no, no . . . let's go and peek through his window and see what he's doing!"

"But he can cast spells!" said Jimmy, looking around him fearfully, spooked by the wild sounds of the wind as it howled through the whipping willows along the road and hissed through the reeds beyond. "He really can cast magic spells!"

His friends laughed. "You'd better watch it, boy. He'll turn you into a bat or toad. Yessir, watch out, Jimmy," jeered Hugh. "He's after you!"

"Shhh!" said Henry. "Aren't you scared?"

"Are you?"

"No, of course not!"

"Neither am I. Let's go! Are you coming, too, Jimmy?"

"But it's dangerous. I'm scared."

"Come on, chicken! There's no such things as witches and magic spells."

"I don't know," mumbled Jimmy. Fearfully he squinted into the howling wind at the faint glimmer of light shining from the small cabin beside the dike. They were getting closer and closer.

The wretched little cabin in the bushes looked lonely and mysterious in the approaching darkness. When the raging wind bore down on it, the cabin creaked on its foundations as if it were groaning in pain and crying for help. And at other times, as if it were muttering threats to drive off anyone who dared to come near. It was a mysterious place, that cabin of Old Abe. And Old Abe himself? He was even more mysterious than his cabin.

When he plodded along the road, grumbling and muttering, no one knew whether the old man was moaning and groaning or if he was cursing and scolding. Just as nobody knew whether his dark eyes were filled with pain or fury, so nobody knew for sure about the mysterious sounds of his cabin.

Behind his cabin were the large peat bogs which turned into a raging, threatening sea when whipped up by a storming wind.

The boys were getting close to the dark cabin—the cabin that groaned in the wind.

The darkness was becoming deeper. High above the cabin, black columns of clouds went scudding by and sometimes a yellow moon appeared like a mysterious ghost through a gap in the clouds.

"Be careful, Henry. No, no! Don't go. Be careful! Please, stay here!" Jimmy begged fearfully.

"Shh! Come on Hugh," whispered Henry.

"Yes, but take it easy. My coffee beans!"

Hugh had gone to the store to buy coffee for his Mom. He and his friends were on their way home when they had spotted the light in Old Abe's cabin.

"Put the bag on the gate post," suggested Henry.

"Okay. You keep an eye on it, Jimmy!"

"No, no, I won't! Please don't go!"

Jimmy didn't dare stay by himself at the old post. At one time the post had held a gate, but it had long since disappeared. No, then he would rather go with the others, no matter how dangerous that might be. To stay behind all alone and maybe have to walk home by himself? Brrr! Why did those two always have to be dare-devils? He would never go with them again. Never!

"Come on back, Hugh!"

Fearfully Jimmy grabbed Hugh's shirt and tagged along.

Creeping through the bushes, across the small yard, the threesome closed in on the small lamplit window which looked like an eerie red eye staring into the darkness. Cautiously, on tiptoe, heads bowed low, they snuck closer and closer.

Splash! Hugh stepped into a hole and fell headlong into a mud puddle. The boys trembled in fright. Had Old Abe heard them?

"Ooh! Ooh!" moaned Jimmy.

"Shhh! Be quiet, dumbbell!" grumbled Hugh, who had scrambled up again.

"Come on, Hugh," whispered Henry encouragingly.

"Yes, let's go. Can you see him? Is he inside?"

"Shhh! Yes, I can see his white hair. See? Just above the window sill. Shhh! Shall we go still closer?"

"Oh, no, no!" moaned Jimmy under his breath. He didn't dare groan out loud. Hugh had already punched him once.

Closer and closer they crept, right up to the window, framed by a thick, tangled growth of ivy. Crouching under the window, they pulled themselves up by the window sill, craning their necks to peek inside.

Even Jimmy's curiosity seemed to overcome his fear. He, too, peered in, just for a second. Then he huddled down again, feeling safer under the window than right in front of it. Getting bolder, the other two took a longer, closer look. They had a good view of what was happening inside for there were no curtains on the windows. After all, how many people came close enough to this lonely cabin set far away from the main road?

"Look! Oh look, Hugh! Look at that!" whispered Henry.

Old Abe was sitting at his table, close to his old-fashioned kerosene lamp. The light falling on the old man's head seemed to turn his white hair into silken silver threads. He was busy with something. In front of him, on the crude table, stood a little wooden box on wheels and without a lid.

"I wonder what's in that box. Give me a boost!"

Hugh hoisted Henry up a little. It was a good thing

that the old man was partly turned away from the window, otherwise he would have noticed the movement outside.

"A doll! Have you ever! A doll! Let me down! Quick!"

The old man moved his head. Did he hear something? Again the boys peeked inside. Old Abe reached into the wooden box and from it he carefully lifted a shabby, worn-looking doll in an old, flowered dress. It was an old, old toy with curls carved into its wooden head; its hair was painted black and its dirty cheeks bright red; and it had only one arm. Carefully, very carefully Old Abe laid the doll on the table. Then his large, coarse workman's hands burrowed into the wooden box again. He seemed to be making the doll's bed. Ever so gently he put the doll back into the box and tucked it under the dirty old quilt. Then the old man slowly pushed the box with little wheels back and forth across the table and on his rugged, weather-beaten face there appeared a strange expression—something akin to a smile.

A smile? The boys were amazed at what they saw. They had never seen Old Abe look like that before. Jimmy, too, risked a frightened glance inside. No one had ever seen Old Abe smile. Everyone knew that he never, ever smiled. And now? Was it really a smile that they saw on his bearded face, a friendly smile, or was it a wicked scowl?

The boys were amazed at Old Abe's smile. For the old man couldn't smile any longer; even when his stiff old lips tried to form a smile, it became a scowl, a strange scowl.

"Eerie, isn't it?" Henry Hoover said softly.

"It's a voodoo doll. It *must* be a voodoo doll!" whispered Jimmy fearfully. "Let's get away from here!"

"No, be quiet! Shhh! Look!" warned Hugh.

Old Abe stood up and, with the doll's bed under his arm, he stumbled over to his bed built into the wall. Behind the tattered curtains covering the bed he carefully hid the old toy.

Suddenly a deep voice sounded from the dike: "What's going on there, eh?"

The boys cringed in fear. The mysterious cabin with the mysterious old man, the dark evening and the wildly gusting wind had already made them spooked and frightened. And now, on top of it, that sudden, awful voice from the darkness.

Jimmy groaned in fear.

Old Abe glanced at the window. It was a good thing that the three peeping-toms had ducked down.

"Get away from there! Right now!"

"Yes, yes! Oh, yes sir!" moaned Jimmy.

"Ha-ha-ha!" laughed the voice from the dike. "Ha-ha-ha! Yes sir! My, my, you guys sure are brave!"

"O-o-oh!" laughed Henry. "It's only Red Roy."

"Whew!" sighed Hugh in relief. The lanky youth standing at the gatepost had given him quite a scare with his angry, threatening voice.

In their fear they had looked around for a way of escape because they had thought that they were facing the village constable. But the only way out led between the gateposts. Old Abe's yard was separated from the dike by a deep ditch, behind the house surged the peat swamp, and deep creeks flowed by the yard on either side.

But it was only Roy Broadfoot, the sixteen-year-old helper of farmer Jackson, a tall, red-haired fellow, known in the village as Red Roy.

Henry recognized Roy's voice. Now the three of them crept toward him. After the scare they had had it was a big relief to see Red Roy standing there. Any other time the boys would rather have had nothing to do with him. After all, they were much younger than he; none of the three were quite twelve yet. And Red Roy had a bad reputation. "He's mean," said the boys of the village. "He's full of dirty tricks," said people who were in a position to know.

Now, however, the boys saw him as an ally. They knew that he always abused and teased Old Abe.

"I saw your heads against the window. What's the old weirdo doing? Never mind, I'll have a look myself."

Boldly he marched up to the window, wanting to show the boys that he's not afraid in the least.

"Shoot! I don't care if he hears me. I ain't scared of him. Just let him try something, that old geezer!"

"Let's go home now. Come on, Henry," pleaded Jimmy. Now that Red Roy had entered the picture he was even more anxious to leave.

"Yeah, in just a minute. Let's have one more look."

Henry and Hugh crept after the newcomer, and Jimmy, in spite of his fear, followed them.

Henry told Roy about the little box on wheels.

"No way!" jeered the boy. "A doll? It's money, I tell you. Gold and silver coins. Lots of money—stolen money. He's an old sneak-thief, that's what he is! I'd like to get my fingers in that box sometime. Wouldn't you, Henry?"

Henry didn't answer. "Could it be true?" he thought.

Again they peeked in. Jimmy hung back a little. He could get a glimpse from there, and it seemed safer.

Old Abe was sitting at the table again. An old Bible lay open before him. Attentively and very slowly his finger moved along the lines. His lips were moving and now and then he nodded his head.

"He's holding the Bible upside down. Just look," whispered Henry who was watching very closely.

"What?"

"Shhh! Shhh! Duck!"

The old man stood up and again he walked to the bed and rummaged behind the curtains for what seemed like a long time.

"He must be counting his money!" said Roy. With a greedy gleam in his eyes, he followed every movement of the old man. "I wish I had his money." Again the boys ducked. Old Abe was coming back to the table. On his outspread arms, he gently carried a child's dress, a wrinkled green dress with red piping. He carried it very carefully, as carefully as a mother carries a baby.

"Will you look at that!" sneered Roy. "He must have stolen that dress, and he's going to sell it. Here, you dirty old sneak-thief! Thief! Thief!"

Wildly Roy banged on the window panes until they

rattled in their frames. Then he ran off, and badly frightened by the sudden daring of Roy the three boys scrambled after him. Across the small yard, past the gatepost, and up the dike they ran.

"Old Abe! Old crook!" Roy yelled when he knew that he was far enough away.

The others said nothing. Sure, they saw some fun in scaring the old man a little, but to call him a thief and a crook? "No," they thought, "Roy is going too far."

Old Abe was badly startled by the sudden noise. In confusion he staggered back for a moment, but then, all at once his eyes flashed and an angry blush spread over his face. He clutched the dress to his chest and glared about the cabin as if ready to defend it against any attack. Then stiffly he climbed up the ladder to the small attic and hid the dress under a bundle of rushes. Then coming back downstairs, he grabbed a heavy stick from a corner of the room and hurried out.

There he stood in the dark night, his chest heaving. Angrily he waved the stick over his head and from his mouth burst threatening sounds that the boys couldn't understand. He stared scowling into the darkness.

From far away on the dike came a voice, faintly now: "You old thief. You dirty old . . . ."

For a long time the old man paced around his cabin.

The wild wind gusting by swept away the dark mutterings of the old man, the angry curses, the words of hatred. Or were they the sounds of an unutterable grief, a deep pain that the old man howled into the howling wind?

Through a gap in the dark, threatening clouds, the yellow moon appeared like a mysterious ghost.

That night Henry Hoover knelt down as usual by his bed in the dark attic. He shivered. It was cold. Yes, but tonight it was very dark too, so frightfully dark in that large attic. And the wind howled threateningly against the window, and . . . and he couldn't get that awful scowling smile of Old Abe out of his mind. It seemed to be looking at him from every corner.

Henry knelt down and prayed. He prayed the prayer he said every evening, but tonight he kept getting confused. Again and again his thoughts kept returning to Old Abe, and to Red Roy, and to the doll, and . . . . His prayer became a mere repetition of phrases.

Brrr! How the wind was howling! The attic window rattled. What if Old Abe came to peek in his window.

Henry shivered in fear. Quickly he jumped into bed and ducked down under the safety of his blankets.

"Thief," Roy had yelled, and . . . .

Oh, he had just rattled off his prayer, not even thinking of what he was praying. That was wrong. Now God would not hear his prayer, of course. And God knows everything. So God also knew that he had been teasing Old Abe. And that, too, was wrong. And now, safe and warm under his blankets, Henry once again began his prayer, softly and slowly.

"Dear Father in heaven, thank you for keeping us safe, and . . . ."

My, was that window ever rattling! Was Old Abe peeking in with his awful face?

"And . . . and . . . would you please . . . ."

Did Old Abe really have that much money?

"And . . . and . . . ."

But no, Henry could not pray. It was impossible. He was so afraid, so uneasy. It was as if God did not want to hear him. Oh, no, he just couldn't pray!

The night was so dark, so hostile and threatening about him.

Was it because Henry's heart, too, was dark and hostile?

2. Cindy

"Henry! Henry!"

"What?"

"Henry! Quick! Come here! Hurry! Listen, it's your little sister, Henry!"

Henry came running and he panted, "What's the matter? What happened?"

"Hurry, Henry! Hurry! It's your sister! Old Abe has got her! Come on, man, hurry up!" cried Jimmy, stuttering in panic. He stood at the beginning of the narrow dike, wildly waving his arms and jumping about impatiently.

With fearful eyes Henry looked down the dike.

In the clear spring morning, the water in the large swamp beyond the reeds sparkled gayly and in the shadow of the reeds lay little pools like black glass.

"Well," panted Henry. "What? Where . . . where is Cindy? Is she . . . ?"

"Oh, Henry, he must be casting a spell on her! I saw it myself. He took her along."

"Who? Old Abe?"

"Yes. He carried her off in his arms. I saw it myself. He's going to bewitch her."

"What? Bewitch? I don't believe in that stuff. But did she go with him, into his cabin?"

"Yes, I think so. I couldn't see that far, and I didn't dare go any closer."

"But he'll have to let her go now! I'm going after her! He better let her go!" There was fear in Henry's voice, fear for his little sister. Henry did not really believe that Old Abe would cast a spell on Cindy. Dad always laughed when the superstitious people of the village talked about witches and warlocks and spells. But still . . . ? What would the old grouch want with his sweet little sister? Perhaps he would throw her into the water. And he, Henry, had been told to keep an eye on her. If Dad, if Mom knew . . . !

Did he hear Cindy crying in the distance?

"He'd better let her go! He'd better!" cried Henry, becoming more and more worried.

With clenched fists, he stormed along the dike to his sister's rescue.

Jimmy stayed behind, scared and undecided. What should he do? Go with Henry? But that would be risky. You never knew what Old Abe might do. Run back to the village, to Henry's Mom? But then Mrs. Hoover would find out that Henry had not been watching his sister.

They had been playing where the main road ran along

the peat swamps. From the edge of the water they had been cutting bulrushes—those heavy, brown, felt-like cattails which would burn like beautiful torches when soaked in kerosene. It was then that little Cindy had wandered away along the narrow dike. There Old Abe had found her and . . . .

Oh, if Henry's father ever found out, then Henry was in for it!

No, Jimmy couldn't run back to the village. But what then? Ah! In the distance a farmer was walking towards him along the main road, carrying two milk pails on a yoke across his back. Jimmy would ask him to help. He should be a lot stronger than Old Abe. But no, the farmer turned into a side road and disappeared behind some bushes.

Jimmy looked about helplessly. Henry had already run up the dike. Once more Jimmy looked toward the village, but everything looked quiet; and once more he looked down the road, but it too was quiet and deserted. Then, gathering all his courage, he jogged along the narrow dike, after Henry. He stopped every now and then, afraid to get too close to Old Abe's cabin, half hidden behind the reeds and bushes.

Jimmy had weighed his chances, but not for a moment did he think of sneaking away and of letting his friend Henry down.

Henry was strong while Jimmy was weak; Henry was daring, while Jimmy was scared; Henry was a daredevil, while Jimmy was cautious; and Henry liked to boss Jimmy around. Perhaps because of all this Jimmy liked Henry very much; he liked him more than any of his other friends.

Jimmy jogged on, fearfully peering ahead of him.

Everyone in the village knew Old Abe; his name was used to frighten little children. All kinds of strange tales were told about him and his cabin. The villagers feared the lonely, silent old man and kept out of his way. The most sensible among them, those who laughed at witchcraft and black magic, shrugged their shoulders about the strange old man. No one understood him, and those who tried to be kind to Old Abe and tried to get to know him a little better, were put off with a gruff, grumpy reply.

Avoided by adults and feared by children, Old Abe lived a solitary life in his own small kingdom—the dark cabin near the large swamp. Only in the town hall was his full name known—Abraham Diephart; and that he could neither read nor write. Before he moved here a few years ago; he had lived in another province, also surrounded by peat swamps, and he had made a living as a fisherman and thatcher. Yes, everyone knew Old Abe; everyone also knew his black boat in which he constantly rowed across the swamp.

The boys of the village knew Old Abe. Most of them had gotten to know him and his stick in a less than pleasant manner. Whatever they did—whether they looked at him in curiosity, or fear, or scorn, whether they called him names or teased him—he was always angry with the boys. "He can't stand children," the villagers said. Whenever even a single boy came near him, his wrinkled, weather-beaten face would twist into a painful scowl, his deepset eyes would flash under his bushy eyebrows, and he would raise his stick threateningly.

The boys, especially the older ones, loved to bait Old Abe, but always from a safe distance. And as soon as he was out of sight, they would tell the strangest stories about the old man. Nearly everyone believed there was some truth to these stories, but nobody knew for sure. No one *really* knew the old man, that is, no one but God.

On this sunny Saturday morning, when the wild wind had settled and the waves in the large swamp were no longer splashing darkly and angrily like the day before but instead were rippling softly and contentedly, like happy children who know their father is not angry, when the rustling rushes were whispering their songs of sunshine and joy—on this sunny Saturday morning, little Cindy skipped merrily along the narrow dike.

She could no longer see Henry or Jimmy, but she was happy anyway. Stepping along all alone, she was having great fun. Little children are like that: they can have fun and be happy without knowing why. She was happy, so happy that she would sometimes laugh out loud.

In her chubby little hand she carried a stick; with it she struck the grass at every skip of her sturdy little legs. Her blond hair gleamed like soft silk in the sunshine. She was singing, too. It was a song she remembered from home, a song Mom would sing with her at the

organ, a song she had only half learned and only half
understood:

"Jesus woves me, yes I know,
fo' the Bible tells me so.
Wittle ones to Him bewong;
They are weak, but He is stwong."

More than those lines she did not know, and when she
came to the end of the song, she started singing it all
over again:

"Jesus woves me, yes I know,
fo' the Bible tells me so . . . ."

Merrily she walked along, ever farther along the
dike.

From among the reeds beside the dike came a rustling
sound. A large hand stirred the reeds, and a gruff face
came into sight; dark eyes peered at the dike, and a
shaky old voice grumbled something indistinct.

But Cindy heard nothing. Cindy saw nothing. Cindy
was happy, very happy but she did not know why.

And the large hand clutching the reeds trembled.
The gruff, deeply lined face of the old man among the
reeds suddenly lit up with a strange gentleness, like a
dark sky that suddenly opens sending a beam of sunlight
sliding over the land. The dark, deep eyes beamed with
joy. A hand jerked at the reeds and the black boat went
shooting through the reeds, and the stocky old man
hastily clambered ashore.

Cindy stood still. She wasn't scared: she was too happy to be afraid. But she did stop singing and put both

her hands, still holding the stick, behind her back. With her big, frank eyes she stared at the figure that suddenly appeared before her, and said, "Ol' Abe!".

After all, everyone knew Old Abe.

The old man didn't hear what the little girl said. He just looked and looked, twisting his fingers awkwardly in his gray beard.

And then a strange tenderness came into his eyes. The hard lines of his weathered face softened and the stiff mouth slowly twisted into a clumsy smile—at least, it was meant to be a smile, although it didn't look much like one. The old man could no longer smile. Then he shyly held out his gnarled brown hands to Cindy, bent forward and gently he said, "Hello, my pretty little lass. What be you doin' here?"

His old, trembling voice sounded gruff as it always did, but underneath the gruff sound of the words pulsed a deep warmth.

Cindy wasn't afraid of the old man. Did she perhaps pick up those warm undertones?

"Ol' Abe, me have pocket an' a hanky," she told him happily, proudly digging a crumpled cloth from the pocket of her dress.

"My lass, my pretty little lass." His hands stretched out toward little Cindy, and she thought that he was holding out his hand to her. So she dropped her stick, and quickly, trustingly she put both of her soft little hands into the coarse, gnarled hands of Old Abe! A strange happiness seized the old man, as if he had been touched by an angel. He was trembling, and the eyes that had known nothing but hardness

and anger for years grew soft and misty.

"My lass, my pretty little lass!" All at once, glancing around as if about to commit a crime, he scooped Cindy up into his arms and hurried off toward his cabin.

A shadow of fear darkened Cindy's sunny face for a moment. The rough, bearded face of the old man is so near now that it tickles her, and his bony brown hand looks so large on her white dress. "No, no! I want go to Mommy!"

"Shhh! My lass, don't be afraid."

Then Old Abe put the little girl down on the rough dirt floor of his cabin and quickly closed the door, as if he had found something precious which he now had to keep safe from evil hands.

"My little lass, aren't you my little lass?"

He had the little girl on his knee, rocking her gently, her small blond head resting against his shoulder. She was overjoyed, for in her arms she held the old doll—the doll with the dirty red cheeks and the wooden curls.

Her fear was gone. That hairy beard and the old man's rasping breath had frightened her at first, but his eyes, those eyes filled with a deep tenderness, had won her over, and now she felt safe and rested her head on his chest.

Old Abe had searched all through his cabin to find something for the little girl who made him so happy. He had looked for something good to eat, something pretty. He had rummaged through the old cupboard. What could he give her? There was a slab of bacon; but no, she wouldn't like that. Cold potatoes? No, that wouldn't do either. No children had ever visited him before, so he had no toys or sweets in the house.

Then it had flashed through his mind: "The doll!" His heart filled with delight. "Yes, the doll! That was the most precious thing he could give her!" And the old man had brought out the shabby toy as if he were handling a precious jewel, a treasure of great price.

Now Cindy was sitting on his lap listening to the friendly chatter of this old man whom everyone feared and tightly hugging the old, one-armed doll.

At first Abe's fond words came haltingly, sounding gruff in his hoarse throat. It had been a long time since he had spent so many words on anyone. But his voice was becoming friendlier and happier, and his words were coming more easily.

Cindy just listened feeling safe and cozy in the old man's arms, close to his gentle voice and to his kind eyes. She did not understand all he said, but she sensed that the old man was fond of her and she loved that feeling, just as a kitten loves to bask in the sunshine.

"My Jenny!" Old Abe said over and over again, his voice trembling. Cindy thought it meant something like, "my sweetheart," or "my honey"—words that Mom or Dad or Henry sometimes called her. She liked it and over and over again she told the old man that she had a pocket with a hanky in it. She didn't know what else to say, and she hugged the old doll against her rosy cheeks like Mom always hugged her in the evening at bedtime. "Issa nice doll, Ol' Abe!"

A great happiness shone in the old man's eyes. His

stern face was relaxed. He no longer looked like a bad-tempered, cross old ogre, but more like a kind, happy grandfather doting over his grandchild. That was little Cindy's doing, but she herself did not know that.

"Yes, you are my Jenny, my little Jenny!"

Suddenly: "Banggg! Crrrash! Someone was pounding and rattling the window panes and then began kicking and banging the closed door.

The shrill voice of a boy, crying in rage and fear, screamed, "Let her go, you devil! Let my sister go! Let her out!"

Little Cindy was terrified. She flung herself against the old man and clutched his beard, the old doll hurtling across the cabin.

And the old man himself? For a moment he remained seated, unmoving, as if turned to stone, his eyes closed in fear. The loud banging has driven all joy from his eyes. But that was only for a moment. Then he leaped up in rage, Cindy tumbling to the floor, crying. Wild with fury, he ran to the door, tore it open, and with a cry of rage attacked the boy who had so cruelly broken in on his happiness. In one moment the old man had changed beyond recognition. His eyes rolled in anger, and he snorted and snarled and waved his clenched fists about. Every feature of his contorted face was once again twisted into the hard, bitter lines of before; he looked angrier than ever. Henry fell over backwards. The flailing fist of the old man knocked him to the ground. Again Old Abe lunged at him, but Henry ducked under the grasping hands and raced off, past the gatepost, past petrified Jimmy, up the dike, away, away! Away from that terrible old man! Away to get Mom, Dad, the policeman! Away to get help for his little sister!

Nervous and frightened Mrs. Hoover came hurrying down the street of the village. Henry had come running, gasping and panting to tell her what had happened, and he had been joined by a ghostly pale Jimmy. Now, together with Baxter, the fat town cop, they were on their way to rescue Cindy.

It was Baxter's duty to keep the village safe, and he had never trusted the Old Abe. He would get the little girl back to Mrs. Hoover, that is, if the old man had not ... well, you never knew about these things.

From between the curtains of the houses astonished eyes followed the frightened Mrs. Hoover and the fat policeman. The town busybodies quickly joined the strange procession. Henry and Jimmy were in the lead. Henry's father wasn't home. In the distance Red Roy came running to see what the excitement was all about. Secretly Baxter made sure that his billy club would slide easily out of his belt. You could never tell. People said that the old man was very strong.

There they went, down the village street, along the main road. Around the corner, where the tall swamp willows met the road lay the narrow dike.

The procession was approaching the corner.

"Shhh! Silence!" Baxter ordered, his voice full of self-importance. Everyone stood still and listened.

"Jesus woves me, yes I know,
fo' the Bible tells me so."

sang a happy voice, and around the corner, came little Cindy, dragging along the old doll by its one remaining arm.

"Cindy, Cindy!" cried Mother.

"The voodoo doll! Throw it away!" screamed Jimmy, and some of the others also eyed the doll uneasily. They would never admit that they were afraid of magic, but they weren't really sure.

Cindy hugged the doll against her to protect it.

"You may keep it, sweetheart," said Mother. She scoffed at the gossip about magic; she knew better. "You come with Mommy now. You mayn't go off by yourself! Where have you been?"

"It's a good thing the child is back," growled Baxter twirling his mustache. "Or else I would have taught Old Abe a good lesson!" Secretly he told himself, "I won't have to go see him now. You never know . . . ."

That day terrible tales were told in the village about Old Abe. He had bewitched little Cindy Hoover with an old voodoo doll, and her foolish mother had allowed her to keep the doll. He had held the child under water for half an hour. He had burned her feet and pulled out her hair. Each story became more terrible and foolish than the one before. And the hatred and fear of the old man grew.

When Jimmy went by Henry's house in the late afternoon of that day to see if he could come out to play, he saw Henry's downcast face at the small upstairs window. A shake of his head was enough to tell Jimmy what had happened: Henry had been confined to his room for the rest of the day.

That night Cindy went to sleep with the old doll in her arms.

"You are my darling," said Mother, "and Daddy's sweetheart, and . . . ."

"An' me is Ol' Abe's Jenny!" said Cindy.

Mother didn't understand that.

That night in the cabin beside the narrow dike sat an old man lost in somber thoughts.

3. Under Suspicion

It was Sunday, a sunny day full of the joy of spring. The familiar peal of the church bells called young and old to worship. And from all sides small groups of worshipers slowly came strolling toward the church, quietly enjoying God's glorious Sabbath morning.

They came along the winding pathways, across the narrow dikes of the peat swamps, in little boats over the wide marshes glistening in the sunlight.

At the church door people lingered awhile making some small talk. Then silently and reverently they entered the cool church.

Also across the dike with the cabin there came a lone churchgoer. He did not linger at the door and there was no reverence in his eyes. As he passed the people at the door, who stepped aside for him, he muttered darkly, gruffly.

He found a place in the back of the church and sat

down, surly and unmoving. A couple of girls sitting nearby, moved over and giggled softly behind their perfumed handkerchiefs.

Gradually the church filled up. Pastor Larens climbed the steps to the pulpit. He saw the old man in the back, and a look of compassion came into his eyes. He had often called on Old Abe and often talked to him. Sometimes the lonely old man would look at the minister with a hint of trust in his eyes, but just for a moment. Each time again the distrust returned to Old Abe's dark eyes.

The preacher felt compassion. Who could understand the dark sorrow of the old man? Who could comfort him? Only God could do that. For the pastor was convinced that it was a deep sorrow that had embittered the old man. So whenever he could, the pastor rebuked the villagers for believing in magic. He always defended Old Abe. But the old man didn't know this, and he distrusted the preacher as much as he distrusted everyone else, and he was just as gruff to him as he was to the other villagers.

But sometimes, on Sunday, Old Abe's hostile attitude changed. Sometimes, on Sunday, when he heard the warm, inspiring words of the man in the pulpit, Old Abe seemed to soften. But only sometimes, for usually he sat there staring ahead dull and surly. He came to church faithfully and always sat in the same pew. He usually avoided people; but in church he seemed to overcome his dislike for them somewhat.

Once Pastor Larens had preached on the text: "Let the children come to Me, and do not hinder them; for to such belongs the kingdom of heaven." Then something strange had stirred in Old Abe. He had risen from his pew and had listened with burning eyes and trembling hands. And then, with a sob he had sunk back into his seat. The other worshipers had seen it. They had talked about it, but they had not understood it at all.

Now from the pulpit came the comforting words: "Come to Me, all who labor and are heavy-laden, and I will give you rest."

Abe heard it. His heart also heard it, and it trembled. Did the Savior Himself touch Abe's heart? Abe's head sank, deeper and deeper. The people thought the old man had fallen asleep.

Henry, sitting beside his father across the aisle, peered at the bowed white head of the old man. "Old Abe's sleeping," he thought.

But Old Abe was awake. It wasn't the preacher's voice that had awakened him, however. It was the forgiving, healing love of Jesus that awakened new life in Old Abe's heart. Still his head sank, deeper and deeper. And again and again the lonely man heard those deeply comforting words: "Come to Me . . . come to Me. . . ."

When he finally opened his eyes the sun's rays streaming through the windows seemed to sing from heaven: "I will give you rest. Come! Come to Me!"

Abe shuffled out among the other worshipers and silently he slipped away.

Red Roy, standing outside the door, pulled at Old Abe's coat. But the old man ignored him and plodded on.

It was seven o'clock in the evening. The solemn music of the psalms carried far across the peaceful countryside. It was as if everything had stopped to listen: the motionless trees, the small houses with their red roofs, the reeds, the glittering little waves on the large swamp. The huge golden sun traveling toward its resting place far beyond the swamps also seemed to stop to listen.

Henry listened too. But he did not know what he was listening for. He was lying on the bank of the narrow dike, near the edge of the large swamp, stretched out on his back, his hands folded behind his head. Through an opening in the rushes he looked across the water, but he did not know what he was looking at.

The evening sun was setting in dazzling splendor. A stream of liquid gold flowed across the water toward Henry, sparkling and glittering. As he lay there with his eyes half-closed, the frolicking flecks of light came dancing between his lashes. Henry was happy inside, but he didn't know why. He wasn't angry with anyone, not even with Old Abe. He couldn't think evil thoughts now, only friendly ones. And his thoughts wandered and wandered until he was hardly thinking at all. He just lay there; he listened, he looked, and he was happy.

The singing in the church stopped. For a long time Henry lay there, thinking of nothing, his head motionless on his folded hands. Then, all at once, he jumped up and started walking along the dike.

Behind him, Jimmy and Hugh were playing beside the main road. They were picking up rocks from one of the gravel piles along the road and throwing them into the water, as far as they could. Jimmy was winning. Hugh was too fat to throw very far.

Henry walked on.

"A knife!" From the grass he picked up a rusty old jackknife. He tried to open it, but it was rusted shut. "It must have been lost by some boy when he was cutting reed-whistles," thought Henry. He threw it down and kicked it ahead of him. Then he picked it up again and tossed it across the reeds into the swamp. The water opened where the knife fell and swallowed it. Ahead stood Abe's cabin. The old man couldn't be home yet; a little while ago the boys had seen him at the other side of the village.

Suddenly an idea popped into Henry's head: he would go and peek into Old Abe's window once again. His curiosity had grown. Now he had the time to take a good look. Far behind him Jimmy and Hugh were also coming onto the dike. Henry beckoned them, but they didn't come any faster. Hugh was still trying to beat Jimmy at the rock-throwing game.

Worried just a little, Henry carefully walked past the gatepost and across the small yard. He tiptoed to the window, and . . . .

"Oh!" Startled he stood still, too scared to even run. The latch of the back door rattled, the door banged open and a face as frightened as Henry's looked around the corner to see who was coming. It was the cunning face of Red Roy. Henry quickly recovered from his shock, but it took Roy a little longer. For a moment his eyes flashed with resentful anger and his hands clenched into fists. Oh, he would like to punch and pummel this kid who gave him such a scare; he would like to kick him into the water. But no, Roy controlled his anger and forced his lips into a grin. Then he ducked back behind the cabin, motioning Henry to follow him. Henry went.

"Ha-ha-ha!" Roy laughed phonily, giving Henry a searching squint. "I thought you were Old Abe!" Then, all at once, he grabbed Henry by the shoulders and snarled, "Don't you tell anyone that you saw me here! Not a word to anyone! If you do, I'll . . . I'll beat you to death!" Furiously he shook Henry with every word. But immediately he changed again. "No, I'm only fooling. But you won't tattle on your friend, will you? Promise?"

Henry, surprised but flattered by the word "friend," promptly answered, "It's a promise!"

"Good! Here, this is for you. But never, ever tell anyone. If you do . . . ." And again a threatening hatred glowed in his eyes.

Then he slunk away, through the bushes, up the dike, and disappeared in the opposite direction from the village. Henry stood there, bewildered. In his hand glistened a silver dollar. "A dollar!" That was a lot of money to Henry. Quickly he hid it in his pocket as Jimmy and Hugh drew closer roughhousing with each other.

But, strangely enough, suddenly his happiness of a moment ago was gone. A vague fear seeped into his heart. Why he didn't know. Why should he suddenly be afraid and worried? He hadn't done anything wrong, had he? He could keep that dollar, couldn't he? After all, it was Roy's. Or . . . or was it?

Then he laughed aloud. But the laugh came from his lips, not from his heart. He grabbed both his friends and wildly he danced around with them. But they didn't notice that he was acting strangely. Henry danced about wildly, but . . . but . . . the coin danced along too. Henry could feel it there, dancing in his pocket.

"Oh! Look! Fire!" Jimmy suddenly shouted. His pale face became even paler.

"Where? Oh, yes! Look! Fire! Fire!" yelled Hugh, too.

It gave Henry a terrible fright, more so than the other two boys. Was that also because of that silver dollar? He trembled. His fear had suddenly become a strange dread, and he himself did not know why. But his throat felt tight and his head throbbed.

Behind the village, black smoke clouds were coiling up into the sky and now and then slender flames shot upward like red and gold daggers.

"Fire! Fire!" screamed Jimmy and Hugh.

"Fire!" Henry screamed too, and he ran along with his friends. He stuck close to them, for he had the feeling that at any moment someone might grab him by the collar.

Lurching along the dike came Old Abe, frightened and flustered. He was walking as fast as his old legs would carry him, and his face was ghastly pale.

Cringing the boys moved aside, but Abe didn't see them. He just hurried on. Henry glanced back as the old man disappeared into his cabin and slammed the door shut.

The entire village was running toward the place where

the smoke was rising and the flames dancing skyward. The fire was at Mr. Jackson's farm. The farmhouse was engulfed in flames.

The three boys tried to squeeze to the front of the crowd, but Jimmy's father spotted his son and made him stay at his side. Henry stayed back, too. Usually he would have been in the front row, but now . . . . No, he kept feeling the silver coin; it seemed to burn in his pocket.

Only Hugh pushed farther ahead. He watched wide-eyed as the village pumper arrived. People brought out ladders and hooks, and with wet canvasses they tried to save the two haystacks.

Everyone who could, lent a hand. The bull and a few

cows which were not out in the pasture, were led out of
the burning barn with great difficulty. Everything that
could be carried out of the house was stacked in the
yard. The mayor himself took command, and Baxter,
the policeman, strutted back and forth to keep an eye on
farmer Jackson's possessions. The fire burned ever fier-
cer. The wild flames danced as if they were mocking the
thin stream of water from the pumper. At times choking
clouds of smoke covered the yard.

And night was falling.

"The horse . . . , oh, the horse!" shrilled a boy's voice.
"Here, here! The horse! Over here!" It was Henry. To
relieve his strange feeling of anxiety he had walked
around the barn to the rear. He had discovered that the

rescuers had forgotten the black horse of farmer Jackson. The horse was tied in a small stable at the side of the barn, all by itself.

"Help! Help!" he screamed again. But nobody listened to the cry of a boy. Voices were shouting everywhere as people called to each other for help. But wait, someone was coming. It was Hugh. In his eagerness to miss none of the excitement, he had kept getting underfoot. He had been poked in the back by one man and boxed on the ear by another because he had stepped on the fire hose. But now he noticed Henry's wildly waving arms. Did he hear Henry scream? Hugh ran toward his friend.

"Hugh, Hugh! The horse! Over here!" shouted Henry.

Then Hugh saw the horse too. For a moment they stood there, undecided. Then they threw the stable door open and tried to untie Blackie. They were greeted by a squealing sound. Crazed with fear the poor animal lashed out with his hind legs; it reared up against the hayrack and tore frantically at the strong halter, but it refused to break. The roof was burning, and a few small flames came shooting from the straw under the horse's hind legs. Another minute or two, and the rising flames would engulf the trampling hooves, climb the heavy legs and the shiny back, and reach for the flying mane and the wildly tossing head.

"Help, help!" the boys screamed. But no one heard. Each second of delay brought the beast in greater danger. But they couldn't enter the small stable; they would be trampled by the horse's thrashing hooves.

"The window, Hugh! Over there!" They dashed toward it.

"Bend over, Hugh!" Hugh obeyed. He had already caught on. They had played "leap-frog" so often.

Hugh stooped down and Henry straddled his shoulders. Then, with a heave, Hugh lifted his friend up. Yes, it worked. Henry could just reach the window. But he had to get still higher. Quickly Henry scrambled up until he was standing on his friend's shoulders. Hugh trembled under the weight. He put his fists on his hips, his chubby red face glowed with the strain and the tip of his tongue stuck out of his mouth.

"A knife, Hugh! Do you have one?"

Hugh had a knife in his pocket. Groaning with effort, he handed it up to his friend. Henry leaned through the window; his hand with the knife groped for the halter rope.

Thick smoke boiled into his face. He coughed, but he kept his head inside, looking for the rope.

Wildly the head of the poor animal jerked up and down. Flakes of lather flew from his sore, open mouth and his large eyes bulged with terror. Over the wild clatter of the hooves sounded a wailing whinny.

Henry touched the rope; he thrilled with joy. He sawed and carved with the dull knife, he hacked, he cut, and he sawed again.

The smoke was getting thicker, and the beast more terrified. Henry sawed and hacked with all his might. He forgot about everything but the tough rope and the dull knife. Higher and higher the flames climbed around Blackie, but Henry sawed and hacked and . . . .

Snap! The rope broke.

The tormented, half-crazed animal leaped back a couple of steps, and then, in a mad rush, it galloped out into the darkness. Sparks still glowed in the singed hair above its hooves, but its mad speed soon put them out.

Henry toppled backward off Hugh's shoulders.

"Good work, boys!" a friendly voice suddenly said behind them. The boys looked up in surprise. It was Pastor Larens.

"Good work, boys! Well done! I'll tell Mr. Jackson you saved his horse."

Hugh looked proud and happy. For a moment Henry, too, felt proud, but then . . . then he felt that awful coin in his pocket, and he blushed a fiery red. What if the preacher could look into his pocket? Should he throw it away? No, he would give it to Mom. That would be good. Or would it? Maybe it was an unlucky coin, thought Henry. Or maybe it was stolen.

The fire was dying down. The mayor had left. A group of people gathered around constable Baxter. The two boys had been reassured by the pastor that Blackie would turn up again. Now they squeezed through the crowd. There, with a wicked grin on his cunning face, stood Red Roy. He had a lot to say, and everyone was listening to him. Baxter, eager to bring news to the mayor, was solemnly taking down everything Roy said. The boys listened too.

Nobody knew what had caused the fire. Mr. Jackson had been in church with his wife when he heard the fire alarm; and Anne, their aged housekeeper, had been dozing in a chair when suddenly someone had banged on the window and shouted that the farm was on fire.

And now Red Roy had come along and told Baxter that he had seen Old Abe sneaking around the farm.

"No lie! And he was lookin' around kinda funny-like, and I saw him feeling the thatched roof. That's a fact! And when he saw me, he run off. I went after him and then . . . then he swung his stick at me. But I wasn't scared!"

The people listened eagerly. Baxter kept writing.

"And then he ran off and . . . ."

Suddenly Roy noticed Henry Hoover in the crowd. He paled, stuttered, and his lips trembled. But he quickly recovered and, looking threateningly at Henry with his green-gray eyes, he said, "Isn't that right Henry?"

"What? Oh yes, yes!" Henry answered hastily. "Yes, isn't it, Hugh? We saw Old Abe run to his cabin, and he looked as if he'd had a bad scare."

Baxter took this down, too, and Henry felt very important, talking to the policeman and seeing it all written down!

"Yes, and he slammed the door, and . . . ." But the coin in his pocket seemed to sting his leg with every word he spoke. "And . . . ."

"I know enough now, folks!" Baxter said gravely. He twirled his mustache, and then went on as if reading from a book: "Justice shall have its day!"

It burned Henry's ears: "Justice shall have its day!"

"We'll arrest Abe! On whose help can I count?" asked Baxter, looking around the crowd. "You never know . . . ."

Baxter wasn't among the bravest.

"On mine!" "Me!" "Me too!"

Many of the onlookers volunteered, eager for a brawl. Twenty strong men should be able to overpower one lonely old man. "Let's go then!"

The procession started out with Baxter bravely taking the lead. The still smouldering farm glowed behind them in the dark night.

"Come Henry," said his father. "Come on, boy. We're going home."

Again the coin stung Henry's leg. Would Dad notice?

"I'll hide it," thought Henry. "I'll hide it in a good, safe place."

When Baxter and his volunteers, a little nervous now, reached the dark cabin along the narrow dike, they found the door locked. So they climbed in through the window. But no one was home. They searched the area around the cabin, but they couldn't find the old man. They yelled and called him names, but there was no answer.

Still shouting names at the cowardly old man and boasting of their own bravery, they trooped back to the village.

"Tomorrow," said Baxter. "Tomorrow!"

Far out on the large swamp, hidden among the tall reeds, lay a black boat. In that boat sat an old man, his face hidden in his hands, as if he were suffering untold pain.

The stars twinkled kindly, like eyes which see much, but say nothing.

4. A Hard Struggle

The next morning Henry stepped out into the street just as the church clock was striking eight. He had already fetched some carrots from the small garden behind the house for his mother and had used the opportunity to hide his silver dollar. He had pushed it into the loose soil with his finger at the end of the row of carrots and marked that spot with a short, red stick. Now he would always be able to find the coin back.

Henry figured it would be safe there. He still didn't know what he would do with the money, but he couldn't keep it in his pocket. When he carried it on him it was always on his mind. And there would be a strange pain in his throat, or in his chest, somewhere deep within—a kind of stab. No, the coin had to go.

That strange feeling wasn't so strong now that the coin was safely buried. Maybe it would go away altogether, and then he would dig it up again.

Whistling happily he strolled into the village, toward school. He had almost an hour to play before school. Had Blackie been found yet? Had the preacher told the farmer about their part in the horse's rescue?

What was that? Listen! Singing! Henry stood still for a moment. Where was that sound coming from? Yes, it was coming from the main road and it was getting closer. Say, wasn't that the tune the soldiers were singing when they marched through the village several weeks ago, on their way to camp? Listen, there it was again:

"You're in the army now;
You're not behind the plow . . . ."

Henry ran toward the singing. Just around the corner of the village street he met the strange procession.

Now, why did he think of that red stake in the garden patch again? Why . . . ?

He shook it off, that awful feeling. Why should he let it spoil his fun?

"Why, look! It's Old Abe!" Henry mumbled to himself, and for a moment he forgot his strange heaviness.

There came Old Abe, his hands tied behind him, stumbling along between Baxter and a policeman from the neighboring village. Around them swarmed at least twenty jeering boys and girls. Even some older people, caught up in the excitement, walked along laughing. Again and again they sang the mocking song:

"You're in the army now;
You're not behind the plow . . . ."

This was exciting. Old Abe was being dragged along by two constables. Look how fast he was forced to go!

And all around him were jeering and singing children. Henry, too, joined in the merriment of the parade, but he felt uneasy about his merriment. He felt as if something very bad, something very sad was about to happen. Henry tried to push his way into the crowd. He wanted to get closer to Old Abe, he wanted to take a good look at the old man. So far he could only see Abe's white hair and his cap perched on his head at an odd angle.

Henry squeezed closer. Then he saw Old Abe—he saw him and he saw the depth of his misery.

Henry stared at the old man in shock. He felt as if he were looking at an open wound or at someone with a horrible disease. But Henry was looking at Old Abe.

Abe staggered along between the two policemen. Dragged along by his shoulders, he stumbled on, his gray head hanging on his chest and his wrinkled, swollen hands cuffed behind his back. Henry moved along, looking at Old Abe.

Now and then the old man lifted his head, and his dark eyes glared about in helpless rage. Then his head sank down again, and the old man shuddered at the clamor around him. His eyes had the look of a wild animal caught in a trap. Garbled sounds escaped his lips. On he plodded, a picture of despair, dragged along by his captors.

And as Henry looked at Old Abe, a strange compassion rose in him, a compassion like he had never felt before.

On they went through the village street, across the church square, past the parsonage. Upstairs in the minister's house a hand pulled a curtain aside. Pastor Larens watched as the noisy parade passed by his house. Some of the boys, glancing up, stopped their jeering. Somewhat ashamed of themselves, they quickly looked down at the street. The adults dropped back a little, acting as if they weren't really part of the mob. Baxter saluted.

Slightly, ever so slightly, the preacher shook his head. Those who noticed it took it as a sign of disapproval of the wicked old firebug. But if they had seen the compassion in their pastor's eyes, they would have thought differently. Abe did not see the preacher. He just plodded on. But his eyes became more and more frightened, and his trembling grew worse.

Henry's compassion grew. The eyes of the black horse had been just as frightened last night in that burning stable. But then he had been able to cut him loose.

Henry was no longer singing along. He could not take his eyes off the old man. Closer and closer he walked to him, as if he could comfort him that way. He saw his heaving chest and heard his labored breath.

He could hardly bear to look at the old man anymore. He would have liked to attack the policemen, push them away, and yank the cuffs off the old man and tell him to run for it. He wanted to save him from his misery, just as he had saved Blackie yesterday. But he did nothing. What could he do? Old Abe was a criminal. Red Roy had said so.

Red Roy? Why did he suddenly think of that red stake again, that red stake in the garden? He tried to push it out of his mind!

The procession moved on. Now it was passing Henry's house. Henry saw his mother standing at the door. Cindy was perched on her arm. Look, Cindy was holding the old doll in her hands, its wooden head hanging down.

Old Abe also saw the child, the child with the doll.

His eyes lit up. Suddenly he straightened up. Alarmed, Baxter renewed his grip on the old man. He thought Abe was making an attempt to break loose. "Watch it!" he said in his most authoritative voice. "Justice shall have its day!"

But Old Abe didn't hear him. Old Abe didn't see him. He only had eyes for the child with the doll. His handcuffs creaked; he wanted to stretch out his hands to the little girl.

All at once he stopped. "Ol' Abe, issa nice doll!" Cindy called out as she recognized the old man. She did not understand the sad thing that was happening to him. Abe's face changed dramatically, a smile played about his lips and tears glistened in his eyes.

But then he suddenly broke into sobs; he hung his head lower and lower. The old man crumbled to the ground.

But he was lifted up again, some of the bystanders jumping in to help. Together they carried him to the police station at the far end of the village.

Henry continued on his way to school. His strange fear of yesterday was back: as if an accident had happened and as if it were his fault. He kept thinking of that red stake. It was like a threatening finger pointing at him. Henry squeezed his eyes shut so that he wouldn't see the stake, but he only saw it more clearly.

The boys chattered excitedly about Old Abe. They told all kinds of mysterious stories about him; what one did not know, the other supplied. All of them were sure of one thing: that morning the mayor and the two policemen had searched Old Abe's cabin, and in a little wooden box on wheels, they had found the gold watch chain of farmer Jackson. A thief had broken into the farmer's house and taken all the money from the dresser, along with his wife's jeweled earrings and the farmer's gold watch and chain. Then he must have put fire to the house to cover his crime. Now they knew who the thief was. Old Abe of course! True, they had only found the chain, but obviously he must have hidden the other things elsewhere. Everyone agreed with that, including Red Roy. Yes, Old Abe was a thief and a firebug.

"It is a good thing that Red Roy has brought it to light," people said. "That boy has pulled some bad stunts, but this time he did the right things."

Henry listened to the chatter. He didn't say much.

Henry had a bad day at school. Early in the day he was scolded for not paying attention. He kept forgetting about his work and thinking of other things. In his mind he saw Blackie jerking at his halter; he saw Old Abe being carried off; he heard Roy whispering, "Not a word to anyone!" And the red stake danced before his eyes. He would work for a few minutes, and again Blackie would come racing across his book, and he would hear Old Abe sobbing, feel Roy grabbing his shoulders and see the red stake rising before his eyes.

The pictures kept whirling through Henry's head. They wouldn't leave him alone. No matter how hard he shook his head, they wouldn't go away; they kept coming back. They upset him and made him feel terribly afraid.

His head felt so heavy. Or, no, it wasn't his head; it was his stomach that hurt. But then the pain seemed to come from his back.

He just couldn't pay attention to his work. He caught himself adding when he should have been subtracting, and dividing when he should have been multiplying.

His teacher noticed his restlessness. He looked at Henry with his piercing eyes and said, "Henry, I think if we could open the door of your heart, some ugly little creatures would come crawling out."

Henry blushed and bent deeper over his book.

What did teacher know about it anyway? Not a single thing. And it wasn't true either! Of course not. He hadn't done anything wrong. That silver coin? But he had come by it honestly.

"What's the matter, Henry?" asked Jimmy, who was sitting beside him.

"Nothing! Don't bother me!" snarled Henry. He scribbled in his book again, and once more Blackie flashed across the page, and Old Abe, and Red Roy, and the red stake. The small stick became a club, a tree, a looming tower that threatened to topple and crush Henry.

"Henry, you're daydreaming again!" warned his teacher.

Yes, Henry had a bad day at school.

At noon he didn't really want to look at the red stake,

and yet he went into the garden. There it was. Henry shivered and walked off.

Oh, why, why did he feel so afraid? It was getting worse and worse! During lunch Dad and Mom talked about Old Abe. Mother felt sorry for him. So did Father, but he also believed that the crime ought to be punished. The old man should not have broken in and set that fire.

"Still . . . I don't quite understand it," said Father. "Poor old fellow! Why would he have done it? That Red Roy, who accused him—he seems more like the type. He could have done it himself. But the evidence was there: the gold chain, the running away . . . ."

Henry seemed to choke on his food; it wouldn't go down. Or was it fear that stuck in his throat? Father's words rang in his ears: "Red Roy could have done it himself." Could that be true? "No! No, it couldn't be!" thought Henry alarmed. "But Roy had acted so guilty when Henry had seen him coming from Old Abe's cabin Sunday evening. But . . . no! No! Old Abe had done it, of course."

Henry's parents didn't notice that their boy, usually a good eater, hardly touched his food. After devotions he rushed out the door, back to school again.

And there his torment started all over.

"Red Roy could have done it himself." His father's words kept echoing in Henry's head. He kept thinking about what had happened at Abe's cabin that Sunday evening. He recalled everything: every word Roy had spoken, the way he looked, his phony laughter, how Roy had grabbed him—every detail. He couldn't drive out that nagging question. It kept coming back: "What had Roy been doing in Abe's cabin?" It must have been something unusual, or else he wouldn't have acted so strange, so scared, and he certainly wouldn't have given Henry that money. Roy must have been doing something bad.

Should he tell Baxter about it? But no! Roy was Henry's friend; he had even given him a silver dollar. No, that would be squealing, double-crossing, breaking a promise to a friend. He had promised to keep his mouth shut, and he would keep it shut.

And why shouldn't he? Of course it had been Old Abe who had set fire to the farmhouse! Henry had seen him hurrying home, pale and scared; and the mayor had found the chain in Abe's cabin. Of course Abe was the guilty party! Abe!

But what about Roy? What had he been doing?

Henry had to stay in after school.

"Henry!" his teacher said earnestly. "Henry, my boy, there's something bothering you. You've got a burden on your heart. I can tell. But, listen, if you don't want to tell me, or your mother or father then tonight, when you're on your knees before God, tell Him. All right?"

Henry felt tears burning in his eyes. He walked away rudely without a "good night." But his teacher understood and forgave him.

That evening a group of boys gathered near the cell where Old Abe was locked up after the mayor had questioned him. Henry joined them. He just couldn't stay home. His mother still hadn't noticed anything. But whenever she spoke to him he jumped.

Now, in the company of the boys, the heavy feeling went away somewhat. They were having lots of fun. They banged on the door, they climbed up to the window, but couldn't see a thing. They shouted and jeered and called Old Abe names. From inside came an angry muttering.

Henry also joined in. He too, banged on the rattling door. He banged so loud and so long that he no longer felt the pounding of his heart. He danced and shouted so loud and so long, that he no longer heard the whispering voice in his heart.

"If only Roy stays away!" Again that sharp pounding, that whispering within him.

Go on! Dance and jump, jeer and shout—that should silence the voice in his heart. More, more! Wilder, louder still, or else he would hear that voice again. "Let's . . . ."

"Baxter! Baxter!" came the sudden warning. The gang scattered. At the church they came together again.

Strolling down the street came Red Roy, his hands in his pockets, a cigarette dangling from his lips.

"There's Roy!" shouted the boys. He was the hero of the day. "Hey, Roy, whatcha doing?"

"Not much," laughed Roy. "I'm taking it easy. I got nothin' to do now that my boss's place is burnt to the ground. Say, are you guys coming along to the old thief's cabin?"

"Yeah! Let's go!" yelled the boys.

"Let's go!" shouted Henry, too. But again that strange fear twisted through his body.

Then he became angry with himself, angry with his own fear. He jumped up and down and hollered as if he were trying to get even with someone: "Yeah! Let's go!"

The gang took off, Roy and Henry in the lead. Down main street they went, along the main road and up the narrow dike. Evening shadows crept across the dike.

Bravely they ran along, swinging their sticks threateningly. Even Jimmy went along; he was a little uneasy about it, but Henry was there too. So he dared to go too.

The crowd boldly approached the cabin, which made a black blotch against the evening sky. Fearlessly they went into battle: more than twenty strong boys, armed with heavy sticks, against a lonely, old cabin in which no one was living.

Roy lagged behind, fumbling with his shoelaces, but Henry ran on. His face was flushed.

"He'd . . . he'd . . . . It was all Old Abe's fault—his troubles at school, his strange fears. He'd . . . he'd . . . ."

Wildly he banged on the door with his stick. His friends shouted their approval, so he beat on it harder still, as if he were beating down his own secret fear. The others, too, attacked the door. Creaking, it flew open.

The boys fell back. Was someone waiting inside? It looked awfully dark inside. But there was no one. Then the boys pushed and shoved each other into the cabin. One boy struck a match.

Roy had snuck around the back of the cabin. He bent

down and searched through the grass. "Ah, here it is!"
he muttered, picking up a brass tobacco case. "I lost this
here Sunday night," he said to himself. "Now no one
will know that I've been here—no one but that meddling
Henry Hoover. But if he dares to squeal on me, I'll . . .
I'll . . . ."

Inside the cabin the boys were turning everything upside down. A window pane crashed to the floor.

All at once Henry couldn't stand it anymore. He had
shouted, but that hadn't silenced the whispering voice

within him. He had banged around with his stick, but still the voice hadn't gone away. He had even cursed, but the voice had only become louder and more insistent.

He ran out through the back door. Startled, he stopped and froze where he stood. Who was that? Over there, between those fishnets hanging up to dry? The dark figure was taking something out of his pocket, very carefully. Now he was trying to look at it, but he didn't seem to be able to see very well. He held it away from him. Just then the moon came from behind the clouds and shone on the object in the dark figure's hand. A watch, a gold watch!

Suddenly Henry recognized the dark shape: it was Red Roy!

Henry felt the blood rushing from his face; he felt dizzy.

"Watch it guys!" a voice shouted. "Someone's coming!" The noisy mob fled, for along the dike came the bobbing light of a bicycle lamp. They scrambled out of the cabin, and up the dike. A farmer came pedaling past the gang of boys. But they didn't return to the cabin; the fun had worn off by now. They went trooping back to the village. Roy, at the center of the group, passed out cigarettes.

Henry was already gone. He was running as fast as he could, far ahead of the bike. Behind him a light bored through the darkness. No, for Henry it wasn't a bicycle lamp. For Henry it was a big, blazing eye, and it was after him. He raced on, driven by panic. He could see it and feel it coming closer and closer, that threatening, burning eye in the darkness. A cold sweat covered his face and his heart was pounding in his throat. He had to get away—away from that eye, that evil eye.

Henry burst into his house, crying with a fear he did not understand. His mother looked at him in shock. "Henry! What . . . ?"

"Nothing! Nothing!" he blurted out, racing up the stairs. His mother, worried, followed him at once. "Henry, tell me please." But Henry said nothing. Still in the grip of his strange terror he flung off his shoes and pants and plunged under the blankets half dressed, pulling them over his head.

His mother, a wise and good woman, sadly shook her head, and went back downstairs. "Later on, when he's a little calmer," she said to herself.

Later, when his father came home, she told him of Henry's strange behavior, and together they went upstairs to see their boy.

"Look. He's sleeping," whispered his mother. "Let's go back down; he'll tell us in the morning."

She saw the frown on her husband's face. "It's all right. Let him sleep. He needs it."

She knew Father. He was a good and kind-hearted man, but he had a temper. And he punished mean pranks severely.

"What has he been up to now, the rascal?" he said. But he, too, whispered so as not to awaken Henry. "Well, let him sleep for now. But tomorrow . . . ."

But Henry wasn't asleep. Trembling with fear, as far under the covers as possible, he pretended to sleep. And when the light of the small lamp in Mother's hand, which she held over his bed, shone through his eyelids, he wished he could disappear.

If Mom or Dad called him, he would—no, he didn't care about the scolding, or the spanking—he would have to tell them everything: about the silver dollar, and about the watch, and about Red Roy, and . . . . Oh, that would be awful!

Between his eyelashes he peered at the rosy lamplight that sent gruesome shapes flitting along the ceiling and then faded as Mother disappeared down the narrow stairway.

Downstairs Mother hung the lamp in the hallway again. A faint glow filtered upstairs.

Henry watched the light disappear. It was a relief for him, and yet. . . .

Oh, how he would have liked to call his father and mother back, and to have them stay close, very close. But no, then they would ask questions, and . . . .

It grew darker and darker in Henry's room, and it grew darker and darker in Henry's heart.

As he lay there quietly in the dark, he saw very clearly what must have happened. For a long time he had run away from the thought that, not Old Abe, but Red Roy was the guilty party, but he dared do so no longer. No, now he understood why Roy had looked so alarmed that Sunday evening when Henry had surprised him. Roy had been up to no good in Abe's cabin. Perhaps it was he who had hidden the watch chain in Abe's room to make it look like the old man was guilty. Yes, maybe. And Roy had kept the watch himself, the watch Henry had seen by the light of the moon a little while ago. Roy must have stolen it from his boss. And the money from the dresser and the earrings had not been found either. Had Roy stolen those too, just like the watch? And could Old Abe be innocent? Would he, Henry, go to jail too?

It seemed as if Old Abe's face contorted with grief was peering over the edge of Henry's bed, as if he could hear the cell door slamming shut. Henry pulled the covers over his head and desperately squeezed his eyes shut, as if those eyes could sleep while his heart could not.

But Henry's heart couldn't sleep. A soothing voice whispered, "Henry, keep your mouth shut! Say nothing! Don't tattle on your friend, your good friend who gave you a silver coin. All you have to do is keep quiet; nobody knows about it. And Old Abe? What do *you* care about him? It serves him right that he's locked up, that mean grouch. Now he can't hit boys anymore. Don't say anything, Henry!"

And Henry did begin to calm down a little. But then, suddenly, it flooded back into his mind: "Roy is a thief! And so are you! You accepted money, and it's because of you, you, you that the old man is in jail, for you and only you know what happened, and you must bring it out in the open!"

Henry tossed about in his bed.

Shhh! From downstairs he heard Mother's soft voice. Was she coming upstairs again? No, she was taking the lamp from the hallway. She was going to bed.

Now the faint glimmer of light from downstairs was gone; now it was totally dark. And Henry's heart was seized with fear.

"Mother! Mother!" he wanted to shout, but the cry stuck in his throat. It seemed as if everyone had abandoned him forever, that he was left all alone in this horrible darkness, that he would always have to stay here and that he would never again see the light. He threw back the covers. He had to get out of here. He would run down to his mother. He had to get away from this dreadful darkness.

But his fear ebbed a little. The small window gleamed faintly. Henry knelt on the bed. And then he heard his teacher's words again: "If you don't want to tell me, or your mother or father . . . ."

Henry bowed his head deep into his pillow and tried to pray. It was a strange and confused prayer, but it was a good prayer—a frightened cry to the Lord, a sincere plea to the only One who could help. It was a prayer from the heart, from a deeply troubled heart. And the Lord who knows the heart heard the confused words that came from the dark heart of the boy in that dark attic.

"Our Father who art in heaven. I'm so scared, I'm so wicked. I've buried a silver coin in the garden, but I don't dare to tell anyone. I promised Roy not to tell on him, and . . . I'm so scared! Oh, dear Lord Jesus forgive us our sins . . . I'm afraid . . . . Old Abe is locked up . . . and Roy will be so mad, and I . . . oh, I don't know, I don't know . . . ."

Then the tears came, scalding tears. His head jerked up and down in his pillow, and between his sobs, he groaned, "I don't know what to do. I don't know . . . I'm wicked, real wicked. I'm a thief. Oh, I don't know, I don't know . . . ."

But the heavenly Father understands tears, too. He even understands groans. And He heard Henry's prayer.

And Henry became calmer. He still shed tears and his breath still came in gasps, but he seemed to shed his fears along with his tears. "Lord Jesus," he prayed, "I'll give that money back, and I'll, I'll . . . ."

Again the question came, "Must I tell on my friend?" But now his fear wasn't so great anymore. Henry could think more clearly now. Again he saw Old Abe between the two policemen. He saw the desperate look in his eyes, and he heard his labored breath.

The compassion returned to Henry's heart, along with a quiet joy. "I'll tell," he sobbed. "I'll tell, Lord Jesus. I'll tell Baxter about Roy, and about my silver dollar. Oh, please, let Abe out of that cell. I'll tell. I'm no longer scared of Roy and of the other boys who'll call me a coward because I tattled on my friend. Oh, I must, I will tell. Old Abe is so unhappy. I will tell!"

And Henry's heart began to grow peaceful, and his mind calm. He had confessed to God now, but not to Baxter yet, or to his mother and father, or his friends. Henry knew that this would still be very hard, and he prayed, "Our Father in heaven, help me that I won't be afraid, that I'll dare to do it, and that Old Abe will get out of jail. Amen."

Then he lay down to think. How would he carry out his plan? How would he give Roy his money back, and how would he tell him that he was going to Baxter to tell all he knew? How would he make it clear that Old Abe wasn't guilty? How would he tell his father and mother what had happened? When Dad found out about the silver dollar . . . .

"No, no," Henry whispered to himself, "I won't be scared anymore. I'll tell everything."

And Henry lay there very still, his hands folded and eyes closed, afraid that the pain and confusion would return if he moved.

Finally Henry fell asleep.

5. Victory

"Henry! Henry! It's time to get up!" called Mother.

Henry woke up with a start. Drowsily he rolled over, yawned, stretched, and . . . cringed! The old fear was back again!

Carefully, like a sick man testing to see whether the pain is gone for good, he looked about the sunny attic, and . . . the old pain flared up again.

But last night, when God seemed so near, when he could ask and tell Him everything, then it had been easy to say, "I'll tell everything that happened!" But now . . . ?

For a moment Henry squeezed his eyes tightly shut, and hid deep under the warm blankets. If he could only hide away from the awful things that lay ahead. How he would love to go back to sleep, to forget all about Roy, and Baxter, and . . . .

But no! Roughly, almost angry with himself, he

69

threw the covers off. With a quick jump he stood by his bed. He clenched his fists and muttered, "I'm ready for Roy!" His eyes looked into the sunny world with determination, and they seemed to say, "I will, I must!"

Henry knelt down for his morning prayer, and when he had finished, he added in a whisper, "Lord Jesus, forgive us all our sins. Forgive Roy, too, and help me so that I'll dare to tell everything. Amen."

He went downstairs. His father had already left. Mother was dressing little Cindy. Mother's soft, searching eyes looked at Henry. He blushed. Mother asked no questions; she only looked. It bothered Henry.

Suddenly he rushed to Mother and hugged her so hard that little Cindy toppled over. He whispered in her ear, "Mother, I've been bad, but I won't do it again, and . . . and I'm going to tell you all about it. I'll tell you this afternoon. Is that all right?"

Mother took Henry's head between her hands, and her eyes looked deeply into his. Henry did not turn his head away. "Yes, I'll tell you everything," he thought. "I'll be strong."

"All right, Henry," said Mother. "You can tell me everything this afternoon."

After breakfast Henry hurried out to the garden. The red stake was still there. This morning it seemed to smile at him. Henry dug up the silver coin, wiped it clean, and walked into the street.

Where should he go first? To Baxter? To the mayor? No, the mayor was too much of a well-mannered gentleman. Henry didn't quite dare to go to him. To Roy . . . ?

"Yes, I'll go to Roy first. He should know what I plan

to do. It would be dirty if I talked behind his back. I'll honestly tell him what I'm going to do, and I'll give him his money back," thought Henry. "But will he ever be mad!"

He would probably find Roy at the Jackson's, in the old barn where the family was living while the house was being rebuilt. Henry would look for him there. He didn't have to go very far. Just outside the village, on the gravel road which ran past the recently burned farm, he saw Roy. The red-haired boy was sauntering towards the village, a cigarette between his lips.

Henry trembled and felt himself turning pale. This was it!

Henry shook his head to get rid of his rising fear. He clenched his teeth, jammed his fists deep into his pockets, and tried to look Roy straight in the eyes. "Don't be afraid, don't flinch," he told himself. "Keep looking at him, open and straightforward."

"What you doin' here?" asked Roy. There was suspicion in his voice. Whenever he saw Henry, he was nagged by a feeling of guilt and a hidden fear.

"I was coming to see you!" said Henry, his voice trembling slightly. But it grew firmer and steadier as he unburdened his heart, "I'm going to tell everything. You stole the watch; I saw it myself. And Old Abe isn't guilty, and he's locked up, and that's not fair. Here's your money back; I don't want it. Old Abe isn't guilty. You set that fire!"

"You're lying!" snarled Roy right into Henry's face. He grabbed him by the shoulders and shook him roughly. "You're lying! You're lying!"

Roy's eyes were filled with violent anger as he looked at Henry, but deep in his eyes there was also fear. What did he have to do to ward off the threatening disaster? He let go of Henry, laughed loudly, and pretended that it was all in good fun. "Ha-ha-ha! That's a good one! Ha-ha-ha!" But in his cunning eyes lurked a hidden fear.

"But it's true! Old Abe isn't guilty! You did it, and I am going to tell! Here's your money. I don't want it!"

When Roy saw that Henry was serious, the fear in his eyes grew. What could he do? Knock Henry down? Kick him, punch him, beat him up? Oh, he'd like to. If only he dared! No, he would try something else first. He dredged up a friendly smile, and sidling up to Henry, he took hold of his arm like a friend and whispered, "Listen, Henry!"

Henry shuddered when he felt Roy's grip and smelled the tobacco on his breath.

"Listen! Here, this is for you! And you can keep the silver dollar too. Here, take it! But keep your mouth shut. If you squeal on me, no one will want to be your buddy."

In Roy's dirty hand gleamed another silver dollar!

Henry tore himself loose, but again Roy grabbed him. Roy saw that the boy meant what he said. He saw it in his determined eyes. Should he knock him down now, give him the beating of his life? No, no yet! And again his fawning voice sounded close to Henry's ear: "Come on, Henry, don't tell anyone. You don't want me to get caught, do you? Come on, Henry, take the dollar! Or isn't it enough? Here's another one, and I've got more of them in my pocket. Come on, Henry, be a sport. Don't tell anyone. Please?"

There was hesitation in Henry's eyes. No, not on account of the shiny coins. He didn't want them. But compassion stirred in his heart—compassion for the pleading boy. He saw the fear in Roy's eyes. He saw the trembling of his hand. But then he shook his head firmly. "No! It's not fair! Old Abe didn't do it, and I've got to tell. I've just got to!"

Roy looked around in despair. He could hardly control his rage any longer. He almost screamed into Henry's ear, "What do you want? You want everything? Here's the watch! Come on, take it!"

Growing furious, he hollered, "What! Don't you want it, you ratfink? You'd better take it! Here!"

"No!" yelled Henry. "No! I don't want anything! Let me go!" He tried to leave.

But Roy grabbed him around the neck and, with a sudden heave, smashed him to the ground. The silver coin rolled across the road into the grass.

"You lousy fink! You think you're gonna squeal on me, do you. I'll kill you first. I'll . . . I'll . . . ."

For a moment, but only for a moment, Henry was scared stiff. But then he was on his feet again, his fists up. No matter; he would rather fight Roy's lashing fists than his pleading voice. In a sudden fit of recklessness, he taunted, "Hit me if you want. I'm going to tell anyway!"

But twelve-year-old Henry didn't stand a chance against his much heavier and much stronger attacker, who, to make things worse, was mad with fear and fury.

Again Roy launched himself at the smaller boy. The gold watch went skidding across the road. Although Henry defended himself valiantly with his fists, swinging and kicking furiously, driven by rage and desperation, Roy battered him to the ground once more.

Henry yelled—not in fear or pain—he just yelled: "I'm telling, I'm telling anyhow! You're the thief. Not Old Abe. I'll tell them everything!" And he fought back even more furiously.

Bumping and wobbling down the gravel road came a big farm wagon pulled by a horse. On it sat a big, strong farmer in blue overalls.

Roy howled in frustration, looking around desperately. He heard the grinding wheels and the thud of the horse's hooves drawing closer and closer. If the farmer heard what Henry was shouting, it meant the end for him. It meant Baxter and jail and . . . . That dirty little fink! It was all his fault. He had nothing more to lose. He'd show that little . . . . The squealing of the wheels stabbed into his brain.

As Henry scrambled to his feet again, suddenly he was looked at the flashing blade of a jackknife. He saw Roy lift it up, aiming for his throat. Henry threw up his arm, blocking the blow.

Again, he tumbled to the ground under the force of Roy's lunge, still crying angrily, "I'll tell, I'll tell anyway!"

A snarl of helpless rage came from Roy's twisted lips. Those wheels . . . those squealing wheels . . . and the big farmer. He whirled, jumped across the ditch and raced away across the pasture.

Henry jumped up. He trembled with relief. The hardest part had been done. He had warned Roy and that part had weighed the heaviest on his mind. Now he could go to Baxter and to the mayor. Now Roy knew what he was going to do; he had warned him openly. Now it wasn't really squealing anymore, was it? No, no it couldn't be, for Old Abe was locked up for something he didn't do.

Henry ran down the road. Down his arm oozed a small trickle of blood, but he didn't feel it. It seeped out of his sleeve over his hand, but he didn't see it. He ran as fast as he could, away from the spot.

The farmer in the blue overalls reined in his horse as he came to the place where the boys had been fighting. He stooped down and there before his astonished eyes lay a gold watch. The farmer picked it up and dropped it into his pocket.

At dusk that evening Henry was sitting at home in the living room. He was peering outside through the window from between Mother's flower pots. He was wearing an old, worn-out shirt. His other shirt hung over the back of Mother's chair, waiting for Mother's needle and thread to patch the hole in the sleeve made by Roy's knife.

In front of the house, Jimmy and Hugh and several other boys were climbing on each other's backs trying to build a human pyramid. Every time the pile collapsed, Henry laughed delightedly. He leaned closer to the window in order to see better; he was kneeling on a chair, and now his nose was pressed right up against the window.

Suddenly the boys stopped playing. Hugh, who was about to try for the top, froze and his jaw dropped as he stared down the street. The other boys crowded around him, hanging over the fence. Jimmy hid behind Hugh's broad back.

Inside the house, a chair clattered to the floor and a half-frightened, half-glad voice cried, "It's Old Abe, Mom! It's Old Abe!"

"Ol' Abe," chirped Cindy from under the table where she was playing with the old doll. She heard Henry's shout and echoed him, but she went on playing without looking up.

The old man came trudging down the street. When he came to Henry's house, he noticed the group of boys and stopped. He shook his fist and mumbled angrily. The boys scattered, and Old Abe trudged on, his head bowed, his arms hanging limply from his shoulders. He was still mumbling and grumbling.

Henry took a step back from the window, as if he were afraid the old man would see him. When Old Abe had disappeared, Henry looked at his mother, his eyes bright with happiness. "Now Old Abe isn't locked up anymore, Mom!" he said. "Now he's free again. Isn't that great, Mom?"

Mrs. Hoover beamed at her boy. Henry saw pride in her gentle eyes.

"Mom, are you angry about my torn shirt?"

"No, not really."

"I'm so glad that Old Abe is free again. Do you think he's happy about it, too?"

"I don't doubt it."

"Can I go to bed now?" asked Henry.

"So early?"

"Yes, Mom. Do you mind?"

"We've had supper. Go ahead. You'll have to get up early, though, to pick some carrots from the garden for me. But don't plant any more red stakes," said Mother with a twinkle in her eyes.

Henry kissed his mother goodnight and charged upstairs. He was undressed in a flash and dropped down on his knees beside the bed. He was still panting. He was extremely happy. He was so happy, he felt like jumping around and dancing and hugging everybody. He was so happy, he felt like sitting still in a corner saying over and over a hundred times, "Old Abe is free, Old Abe is free. . . . I'm not scared anymore . . . I'm happy, happy, happy!" He was so happy, he hadn't been able to stay downstairs in the living room any longer. He had to be alone so he could close his eyes, which were burning, burning with happiness. He was so happy he just had to tell God about it. God had helped him to tell the truth and God had made him so happy! "Old Abe is no longer in jail. He's free!"

Henry said his evening prayer quickly and without hesitation, as if in a hurry to get to the end. A couple of tears burned behind his eyelids when he added in a soft whisper, "Oh, dear Lord Jesus, I'm so glad that Old Abe is free now, and that I've told everything, and that I'm no longer afraid. Thank You, thank You very much! And, dear Lord, forgive the bad things I've done. Forgive Hugh too, and Jimmy and the other boys, and . . . and Roy too. I'm so happy, so happy, so very happy. And I'll always love You a lot, and also Dad, and Mom, and Cindy, and everybody! Amen."

Then he dove under the blankets and curled up, hugging himself happily. Downstairs Mother lit the small lamp in the hallway, and the faint glow that filtered upstairs was like a friendly greeting in the darkness of the attic.

For a long time Henry lay quietly staring at the friendly glow. Sometimes, briefly, he was bothered by the thought of Roy, and the knowledge that he would have to pay dearly for stealing and for setting the fire. But the happiness in his heart always won out. "Old Abe had been innocent, and now he was free!"

When Henry finally fell asleep, there was a big, happy smile on his face. It was the smile of a happy heart in which darkness had been replaced by peace.

It had been an exciting week in the village: first there had been the fire and the discovery of the theft, then the arrest of Old Abe, and now his sudden release. The villagers had a lot to talk about.

Soon everyone knew what had happened. The story was being passed around that the boy of Hoover, the carpenter, had come to Officer Baxter to tell him that, not Old Abe, but Red Roy was the guilty one. Mrs. Baxter had had to bandage the boy's arm because he had been stabbed during a fight with Roy.

Baxter had notified the mayor, who had ordered the immediate arrest of Roy.

But Roy had already flown the coop. A search of the village and the surrounding countryside turned up nothing. Efforts to find the young hoodlum in neighboring villages also met with no success. Now the police in the big cities were on the lookout for Roy.

Farmer Jackson's shed, where Roy had been living, had been searched and the search had produced absolute proof of Roy's guilt. In the chest with Roy's clothing, Baxter had found two big apples. He had accidentally dropped one on the floor, and to his surprise, the apple had broken open and a small wad had fallen out of the hollow center. Inside the wad, Baxter had found one of the stolen earrings. Its mate had been found in the other apple.

Farmer Jackson told the policeman that he had often seen Roy hollow out apples and fit the pieces back together so artfully, you couldn't tell they had been cut. His voice was filled with disappointment. He had been shocked when he heard what Roy had done, for he had been good to the boy. He had taken him in when the boy's mother had died. His father, a wanted man, had fled the country many years ago. Mr. and Mrs. Jackson had treated the boy as if he had been their own son. It hurt them badly to see how Roy had repaid their kindness.

The old chest had yielded even more evidence. Jackson's money was found in the cover of an old book, and in one of Roy's pants pockets was a partly-burned handkerchief that smelled of kerosene. It was wet and dirty; Roy must have retrieved it from the ashes of the burned house and had not yet gotten a chance to get rid of it. Mrs. Jackson identified it as one of Roy's handkerchiefs. Roy had wanted a lot, but he had been too lazy to work for it, the farmer and his wife admitted sadly.

Old Abe had been questioned again, and again he had remained silent. But when the word "fire" had been used during the questioning, he had looked around in panic and become very agitated. Tired of getting nowhere, the mayor had finally said, "The old fellow doesn't seem to be quite right in the head. There doesn't seem to be any reason to keep him locked up. We'll let him go. One thing isn't clear yet. Why did he run off to his cabin when the fire broke out, and why did he seem so frightened then? We'll have to keep an eye on him, Baxter."

"As you wish, your honor! You never know," Baxter had replied.

So just before dusk, Old Abe had regained his freedom.

No one ever saw Red Roy again. One of farmer Jackson's hired hands said the boy had once boasted that escaping from the law was easy. "You just go to a big harbor town and hide in the hold of a large ship," he had said, "and you don't show yourself until you're way out on the ocean. When you arrive in some foreign country, where nobody knows you, you sneak off. It's easy!"

Perhaps that was how Roy had escaped.

That night, when everyone in the village was sleeping, a lonely old man sat in the dark cabin near the peat swamp. His tired head was cradled between his hands and his elbows leaned on the rickety table. His face was contorted by bitter anger and hatred, and he mouthed indistinct curses.

He had returned home to find his cabin in a shambles. The doll's bed lay under the table, one of its wheels broken off. The little child's dress dangled over his bed, torn to shreds.

Then the old man had pounded the walls and sobbed in helpless rage and grief.

Now the shabby, torn dress lay before him on the

table. Old Abe stared at it with mournful eyes. He stared at the tear in the rumpled dress like a mother looking at her injured child. His eyes darkened with grief and his mouth twisted with pain.

Who could comfort this old, lonely man?

The cool night breeze, blowing through the broken window pane, gently ruffled Old Abe's silvery hair.

6. Pastor Larens

During the first weeks after Old Abe's release, the people of the village had been friendlier to the old man than before. Their gossip about him had been less scornful and their thoughts a little kinder. The young boys had stayed out of his way or kept their silence when they had met him, only glancing back after he had passed. The women had even said "hello" to him, and there had been pity in their eyes.

But Old Abe hadn't noticed their friendliness. In gloomy distrust he had gone his way, even grumpier than before.

The sad incident had left its mark on the old man: his hair seemed whiter, his cheeks more sunken, his head more bowed than ever before, and his eyes showed the bitterness in his heart.

"Those boys! Those boys!" he would grumble; and there was a threat in his voice, and in his eyes, and in his clenched fists whenever he saw them—when they came too close to his cabin, when they met him on the street, when they eyed him fearfully, and even when they scurried out of his way.

Boys! Old Abe hated them. But nobody knew why.

And the friendly attitude toward the old man didn't last long. "It's no use!" people said. "You can see the anger in his face. He must have led an evil life. Who knows what he might be hiding."

And again gossip, sinister and foolish gossip, was spread about the old man whom no one understood.

The boys also lost their respect for Old Abe when they noticed that he was even grumpier than before his arrest. They didn't understand his anger at all.

"Why does he have to be such a grouch?" they asked. "Why did he have to beat Hugh with his stick when he had accidentally fallen in front of Old Abe's feet while they were playing leapfrog? Why did he chase them away from the dike when they were fishing for tadpoles and weren't even thinking of Old Abe? Why? Because he's an old grouch, a mean brute! That's why!" And the boys no longer kept out of his way. They baited him, and teased him, and made fun of him.

Old Abe became even more lonely. He lived alone in his cabin, listening to the monotonous rustling of the rushes and the whispering of the wind across the swamp, alone with his sorrow—the sorrow that no one knew, but God.

And nobody understood him.

Shortly after Abe's release, pastor Larens came to visit the old man. He found him deep in thought, sitting on a pile of fishnets that needed mending. With a start, the old man struggled to his feet. There was distrust and fear in his eyes. The preacher's friendly voice vainly tried to put Old Abe at ease. The old man stared at his visitor fearfully, as if he expected something terrible to happen.

The pastor told him of Henry Hoover's honest efforts to clear him of suspicion and the friendlier mood of the villagers. But the old man didn't grasp the meaning of the kind words. He had suffered too much, and his weary head had spent too much time thinking about that one thing. He just wasn't capable of understanding much anymore.

The pastor talked earnestly of God's faithful, fatherly care, and of Jesus' love for even the greatest of sinners, of His comfort and help for the sorrowful. For a fleeting moment those words sounded like music to the old man's ears, and a strange peace seemed to enter his heart. But it was only for a moment, like on Sunday mornings, when the organ music temporarily cheered his heart. Then, then an angry, spiteful look of distrust again settled on his face. Yet, deep in his eyes, there was no anger—only fear and helplessness.

The preacher had seen that the old man's anger and distrust were just a way to cover his deep sorrow. He had come to confront, not his hate, but his misery.

"Abe," he said, his voice filled with compassion, "Abe, you're carrying a great sadness, a deep sorrow. It fills you with hatred toward people, it makes you angry with young boys, and it also makes you rebellious against God! That's not right Abe. I don't have to know the cause of your sorrow if you don't want to tell me. But God should know, Abe. You must tell Him."

Then, to express his compassion, the minister put his hand on the old man's shoulder. A shudder passed through him and he stumbled back, fear in his eyes—the fear of a tormented animal.

"Eh? Wha-at?" he stuttered. Stumbling over his nets in his haste, he lunged out the back door to the small dock where his black boat was tied.

That hand, that hand on his shoulder. It had hurt. It had burned into his heart.

What was it about that hand? Was it the hand of a policeman come to seize him? Were they cruel fingers digging into his flesh? No, it had been the pastor's hand. He knew that. But . . . but it had to be phony, a trick. Who wanted to touch him, Old Abe? No one. People shunned him, feared him, hated him, and he hated them too—all of them. No one had ever touched him during all these long years. And now? The pressure of that hand burned on his shoulder, it burned into his heart.

"I must get away!" he groaned. He stepped into his boat, pushed off and rowed away as fast as he could.

Dumbfounded the pastor stood there, watching the old man disappear behind the rushes. Sadly he shook his head and muttered, "Poor fellow! I sure can't reach your heart. Only God can do that. I'll pray for you!"

Old Abe kept on rowing until he was far out into the swamp. There he allowed his boat to drift into the reeds,

and there he sat deep in thought, staring ahead but seeing nothing, his tired arms resting on the oars.

He had rowed as fast as he could to get away from that man and from that hand, but now he didn't quite understand why he had been so afraid. He could still feel the gentle touch of that hand on his shoulder urging him to come back, and to listen—to listen to those beautiful words and to that voice which he just didn't dare trust. Now the hand didn't hurt anymore; it only urged him to come back.

As he sat in his boat on the lonely swamp pondering what had happened, he felt a strange longing to row back to that man, to feel that hand on his shoulder once again, yes, even on his head, to sit completely still just listening to his voice speaking about Jesus. Then the joy he had felt would come back too. The old man thought he was yearning for that hand and that voice, but his soul was thirsting for much more, for deliverance, for the Deliverer who alone could set him free from his sorrow and give him eternal joy. But he did not yet understand his own yearnings.

Abe rowed back. He stepped back onto the dock, shy and fearful, like a child coming home after hurting his father.

He found his cabin empty. Gone was the gentle hand and the soft voice, the voice that had admonished him. And was that miraculous joy he had felt gone too—gone forever?

Now there was no one there to bring him that still joy. No one. He was alone, and for the first time in a long time he felt his loneliness and his misery.

He sank down on a chair, pondering again. The yearning was still there, but he didn't know what he was yearning for.

The pastor had talked about Jesus. Abe dug out his old, dog-eared Bible. There he could find peace and comfort. He had heard the pastor say that so often on Sunday mornings, and he had said it again. It had stuck in his mind. He turned the pages and searched through the old book. But Old Abe couldn't read. And although his finger moved along the lines and his lips moved, his eyes did not see and his heart did not understand. He was like a blind man seeking gold dust in a pile of sand. His weary head sank down on the old Bible.

There was a prayer on Abe's lips and a prayer in his heart, a strange, confused prayer filled with hate and distrust, with misery and loneliness and longing. It was a plea for mercy, but at the same time it was beset by bitter doubt. Would Jesus listen to his prayer? No, Abe knew very well he couldn't pray as he ought, for he always kept thinking about his hate. He would love to stretch out his arms to the Savior, but give up his hate? No, that he couldn't do. That hate held his heart like an iron fist, the heart that thirsted for peace. That fist strangled all his peace.

The hate won out. Abe muttered somberly. Again that old grief was before his eyes and his mind was filled with those who had caused it.

Those boys! Those boys! The hands that had yearned to stretch out for mercy now clenched in anger, and the voice that had yearned to plead for grace now cursed. Hate had won out.

He sat all alone in his lonely cabin. But the loneliness in his soul was his greatest agony. But Old Abe didn't know that.

It was early fall. At dusk one evening Abe came trudging through the village. He had sold a few bundles of reeds in town, and was now on his way home.

He was seldom seen in the village anymore. He came only to buy food and to sell his fish and reeds. He shunned the villagers more and more. But every Sunday morning he sought out his dark corner at the back of the church. No one else ever sat there. "You have to leave him something!" people said. They would tap their foreheads and say, "He's not quite there."

Slowly he trudged through the village that evening, leaning heavily on his stick. He seemed lost in thought, taking no notice of what was going on around him. There was no one baiting him that evening, no one calling him names and no one tugging at his coat. Yet, whenever he heard happy voices or laughter, his eyes flashed and he stood still for a moment. Then he would plod on again.

At the corner of the street, he suddenly stopped. It was quiet there that evening. Old Abe had seen

something that had caught his attention. His bowed back suddenly straightened up, a strange, gentle expression came into his eyes and his lips twisted into something like a smile. His stick fell to the ground and his hands reached out ahead of him, trembling.

His hard, angry face was softened by a deep tenderness, and with a quavering voice he whispered, "Jenny, my Jenny!"

He stood as if nailed to the ground. His old legs refused to move. With a surge of joy his heart went out to the pale little creature playing in the middle of the street in front of Hoover's house. It was little Cindy.

Mrs. Hoover had undressed her little girl and gotten her ready for bed. She had let Cindy play in the living room in her bare feet and nightgown for a few minutes while she went into the kitchen. Carrying old Abe's one-armed doll, little Cindy had gone skipping down the hall and peeked out through the half-open front door. She hopped in and out, squealing in delight, pretending that someone was trying to grab her by the legs. Mother was staying in the kitchen quite a while. So Cindy paddled down the walk in her bare feet to the open gate. Still playing, she ventured farther and farther out into the street.

All at once, the old, one-armed doll slipped from her hand, and when she picked it up again, two buttons on its woolen dress had come undone.

The old doll with its wooden curls and painted cheeks was Cindy's favorite toy. Mother had knit a woolen dress for it and Cindy was as proud of the new dress as she was of her own white Sunday dress with the red ribbons. But now two buttons had come undone on the back and that just wouldn't do. She hugged the doll against her and tried to work the buttons back into the buttonholes with her chubby little fingers. They wouldn't go. Getting impatient, Cindy forgot she was out in the middle of the street in her bare feet. All she thought about was those buttons that wouldn't go where she wanted them to.

"Bad button!" she muttered. She didn't see anywhere to put down her doll, so she laid it face down on the street and knelt beside it on her bare knees. Again she started fumbling with the "bad button." The tip of her tongue came peeking out of the corner of her mouth.

That was how Old Abe saw her: kneeling in the middle of the street.

"Jenny, my Jenny!" his voice trembled.

All the gloom and anger had gone from his eyes. He gazed at the pale little creature in the middle of the street with deep tenderness. It was the same little girl who had sat on his knee once before, her small hands tickling his beard and that doll was the same doll he had given her.

Then some nasty kid had pounded on his window and frightened the child. Those boys had robbed him of that brief moment of joy too.

Here she was again, the same little girl—his girl. His arms stretched out toward her. But unaware of anything else Cindy fumbled with her doll.

Suddenly, in the distance, there sounded a dull rumbling sound. Chugging and sputtering it drew closer. The shrill blast of a horn shattered the stillness and a black old car swerved into the street traveling at a fast clip. Old Abe didn't hear it until it was almost there. He saw it come speeding down the street in a cloud of dust. A terrible spasm of fear passed through him. "My Jenny!"

"Stop! Stop!" his hoarse voice shouted. "Stop!"

But the car went jolting by him as he stood on the corner. The driver couldn't possibly stop the old car in time.

Another three, two seconds and the big black machine would be on top of the child. Abe saw it coming but could do nothing. He waved his arms frantically. "Stop! Stop!" His knees buckled and dizziness swept over him. He swayed.

"My Jenny!"

In terror he watched it happen—a wild, whirling confusion that scrambled together in his mind. The skidding, shuddering car. A cloud of dust. The fluttering nightgown, shouting, screaming voices. And two long, black arms reaching, reaching and grabbing. Abe watched, and in his terror he, too, wanted to throw himself into the wild scramble in order not to see, not to know. His hands groped for support; he almost collapsed. But he summoned all his strength and fought off his sudden weakness. He forced open his eyes.

Jolting and stuttering the car came to a halt. The dust settled, and beside the car stood Pastor Larens.

His face was pale, his lips were trembling, and his hat lay somewhere in the middle of the street, but in his arms was Cindy. The frightened little girl had both arms around his neck, and her bare feet were thrashing against his black coat.

The preacher had been walking past just as the car had turned into the street. Abe had not noticed him, for he had had eyes only for the little girl. When the car had almost been on top of the child, it had been the preacher's desperate grab that had saved her.

The black arms Abe had seen in the confusion were the preacher's arms.

The driver mumbled his excuses, and Pastor Larens nodded his understanding. He was carrying Cindy through the little gate when her mother came rushing out. A small group of people gathered but Cindy had already forgotten her fright. She was looking for her doll.

"Dolly gone! Dolly gone!" she cried, bouncing up and down in the preacher's arms. Stretching over his shoulder, she tried to catch sight of her one-armed toy.

A neighbor boy picked up the battered old doll for her. It had been flung to the side of the road by the car, and now its one remaining arm had been half-torn off too. Cindy didn't notice, however, as she happily hugged the shabby toy. She knocked its wooden head against the pastor's nose and started fumbling with the buttons again.

"Issa nice doll. Issa nice doll!" she chirped.

Abe saw the little white figure bouncing in the preacher's arms; he saw the curious neighbors gathering around and heard their questions and comments. But Abe didn't absorb any of this. Leaning against a post, he stared dazedly at the small crowd in Hoover's front yard.

One thing he understood; one thing he understood very clearly, and it filled him with great joy. He understood that those black, snatching arms had been the pastor's arms, and that they had saved "his Jenny" from that horrible danger.

The pastor's arms! A great happiness bubbled up in Old Abe. The pastor's arms! They had reached and grabbed; they had done what Abe had been unable to do. They had saved Abe's little girl.

When the old man finally trudged away, unnoticed, in the direction of his cabin, there was unspoken gratitude in his heart toward the man who had done what Abe had wanted to do and who had shared the terror and joy of that horrible moment.

Yes, the old man was now convinced: this pastor who had shared his terror and his joy had to be his friend. Abe's heart, so long hardened by hate, struggled with this strange feeling. His friend! Old Abe had felt it when he had seen those arms reaching and grabbing. Yes, the man who had done that must really love the child. He must love her as much as Abe himself. And the man who had saved the child must also be able to understand Abe's great sorrow.

The thought passed through Abe's mind, "If only he knew about my Jenny!" In his heart, the old man blessed the pastor in silent gratitude. For the first time in many years there was something like love for another person in Old Abe's tormented heart.

Deep in thought, he stepped into his cabin. A quiet joy remained in his eyes. He had a friend, a friend who could understand what it meant to carry a great sorrow, as he had done for so many years. Abe lit the lamp. The small flame flickered and smoked. By its weak glow he again began leafing through his Bible. The Bible was the pastor's friend, so it had to be his friend too.

But soon he was cradling his head in his hands again, and the old, dark thoughts began coming back. True, the pastor had saved the child, and that was good and courageous. And he had taken the child in his arms. But Abe's arms had been empty; he hadn't been able to hug a child to his breast. "Jenny, my lass," he murmured. And for a moment he felt envy toward the preacher who had carried the little girl in his arms.

He had no child to carry in his arms. No, never again would he have a child to carry. All he had was a torn old dress. But his child was gone.

The old man slumped forward over the table and tears burned in his eyes. "Jenny, my Jenny!" he sobbed.

His little girl was gone. She had been gone for many years. But long ago, when she was still alive, then life had been good. Then he had been happy.

But that had been long ago, when he had been living in another house at another peat swamp, far to the east. With him had lived his daughter and her child. Yes, that had been long ago when he had still been happy.

His wife had been dead and his daughter's husband too. That had been sad, but the three of them had been left together and they were happy—he, his daughter, and her deaf and mute little girl, Jenny. Long ago. Yes, they were happy.

"But those boys, those boys!"

In those quiet evenings long ago the Bible lay on the table too. And they read from it every evening, for his daughter knew how to read. Then the little girl would sit on her grandpa's knees and tickle his black beard with her little hands. They had known peace and happiness in that cabin. Long ago.

"But those boys, those boys!"

Abe's anger returned and he squirmed restlessly. He could feel the rage rising from deep in his heart. "Those boys!"

One evening, at dusk when the sun was sinking into the far end of the swamp, he had been fishing far from shore and from his cabin. In the cabin his daughter lay in bed. She had broken her leg in a fall and couldn't move around because her leg was in splints.

That evening a group of boys had come. He could still hear their shrill voices and see their flailing arms. Abe's hands balled themselves into fists. They came and in their boisterousness they built a fire close, too close, to his cabin. He saw it from his boat, and yelled and threatened, but they only laughed. Then he saw the flames spread to the cabin and climb up to the thatched roof. He screamed and howled in terror. And then they ran away, frightened by their own carelessness. They didn't know about the helpless woman inside. But he did. And he saw the flames dancing around the windows and leaping up on the crackling roof. He saw it, but he could do nothing. He rowed like a madman, but when he got there, it was too late. She was dead, suffocated by smoke.

"Those boys! Those boys!"

The old man rose from his chair. The painful memory had unleashed all his anger. Gone was all his gentleness. Gone was all his peace. Hate flared in his heart and in his eyes.

The flame in the lamp flickered. Old Abe shook his clenched fist towards the unseen enemy, and on the white wall behind him appeared a gigantic, threatening fist. It seemed to be aimed at the old man himself, ready to crush him.

Fire still created terror in Old Abe. The call, "Fire! Fire!" still stirred up the old fear in his heart.

On that Sunday evening, when Jackson's farmhouse had burned down, Old Abe had been fleeing from his own painful memories and had tried to forget them by rowing out into the dark swamp.

"Those boys! Those boys!" If only they had left him his little girl, he would not have become so dreadfully unhappy.

After that fire long ago, he had rebuilt his cabin for himself and his little Jenny. He had cared for the girl like a mother. Jenny could not hear, but she understood the language of her grandpa's eyes. She could not speak, but the old man understood each strange sound and each gesture the child made. He had pampered her and loved her more than life itself.

"My Jenny, my little lass!"

"Those boys! Those boys!"

Again boys had come—wild, roughhousing, unthinking boys. Maybe they weren't the same boys who had set fire to his cabin, but they were boys nevertheless, boys with the same shrill voices, the same noisy exuberance, the same recklessness.

They came on a sunny morning while he was out cutting reeds on the large swamp, and the little child was playing on the sloping dike near the water.

They came, a large gang of them, roughhousing as they came along the dike. They shouted at the deaf-mute girl. She, of course, hadn't heard or understood them. She must have looked at those wild boys with large, frightened eyes, hiding her doll behind her back as if to protect it.

They were close to the child when one of them gave one of his friends a playful push towards the swamp. He fell back against the girl, and she was knocked backwards into the water.

Abe saw it all happen from where he stood in his boat. A horrified scream tore from his lips and across the water. Terrified, the little cowards ran off. One of them hesitated for a moment and tried to grab the child, but the mad, roaring figure in the approaching boat scared him off.

Thrashing wildly among the reeds, the little girl drifted away from the shore. Coughing and moaning, she tried to spit out the inrushing water. Then she sank.

Old Abe came and fished his Jenny out of the water. He carried her to his cabin like a mother carrying a sick child. He rocked her in his lap, his little girl with her pale cheeks and blue lips, with her long, dripping hair. He squeezed her to his heart and hugged her in his arms. And stunned with grief, he kissed the pale, cold little hands, the hands of his dead little girl.

This was Old Abe's secret. This was the sorrow that had made him a solitary, a bitter, angry old man. This, too, was the root of his love for Cindy, but also of his hate for all boys.

The old man had risen. His body shook and he raised his fist high into the air. The gigantic fist behind him rose up too, looming above him.

Then Abe collapsed forward onto the table and his breath came in great sobs. Old Abe wept.

What he had seen that evening on the street had raised all those horrible memories of long ago with painful clarity. When the car had come hurtling at little Cindy, it had been as if he were once again seeing his own girl snatched from him. And the same inexpressible pain of long ago had threatened to break his heart.

But those black arms had saved her.

Again those arms appeared before his eyes, and he wept, wept bitterly.

If there had only been such arms on that morning, long ago, to snatch Jenny from the water! If . . . yes, if that pastor had been there *then*! He could have helped. Yes, he understood this grief, this awful grief that wouldn't leave him. No one understood, no one but the pastor!

The old man looked up. If only the pastor were here now. He would understand. He would put his hand on Abe's shoulder again, and on his head, and the pain in his heart would be gone, if only for a while.

But there was no one in the darkening room but Abe. He was alone, alone with the torn little dress. Those boys had done that!

Those boys! Aah! Again the anger flared up in his heart. But he fought it. If the pastor were here—oh, that he were!—he would silence that anger. "Abe," he would say, "it's wrong. Abe, you must bring your sorrow to God. You must!"

But those boys, those boys!

The old man shook his gray head and his weary body as if to shake off the fetters of hate. Pray. That was what he had to do! Tell God about his sorrow.

He folded his hands and squeezed them tightly together as if he were trying to strangle his anger. His lips moved, but he couldn't pray. It would have been easier to curse.

He saw groups of wild boys dancing around him in a wide circle. They were carrying fire and little dresses which they tore into shreds. They called him names and taunted him.

No, the old man couldn't pray. He saw his own evil heart, and trembled.

Once more his head sank down onto his arms, and in great fear he sobbed, "Oh, Lord Jesus, I'm so wicked! So wicked!"

In the darkness outside the reeds rustled in a soft breeze.

7. On the Dark Swamp

It was fall. A blue haze floated over the swamps, and occasionally a gust of wind drew a mournful whisper from the sighing rushes. In the gray distance dark storm clouds gathered.

One day after school three close friends, Henry, Hugh and Jimmy, were playing along the narrow dike. Not far away lay Old Abe's cabin, dark and mysterious.

The boys stopped and stared at it. "I'm not scared at all!" said Henry, suddenly. "I'm not, either," said Hugh. "Yes, but," said Jimmy, "if he ever catches you . . . ."

"Come on," laughed Henry. "We're not doing anything wrong now. I'm not afraid at all. Do you know who is afraid? Old Abe, that's who. Twice I've seen him run away when some boys got near him."

"Yes," said Jimmy, "but . . . ."

Slowly the boys sauntered closer.

Yes, the boys had noticed Old Abe trying to keep out

of their way, even though he looked as angry as ever. They thought the old man had become afraid of them. They didn't know that Old Abe was afraid, not of them, but of himself. He was trying to run away from the anger that flared up inside him whenever he saw any boys. He didn't fear the taunting boys but his own angry heart. None of this the boys knew. How could they?

All they thought about was playing and having fun, sometimes at Old Abe's expense. They never thought about what it was like to be old and lonely. And sometimes when a small voice inside them told them that their teasing and name-calling was cowardly and sinful, they excused themselves by saying, "It's his own fault; he's such a grouch!"

Only a few days ago, he had come after them with his stick, just because they had looked at him with a smirk. They had fled into the fields over a plank serving as a footbridge over a ditch. Stopping, Henry and Hugh had quickly shoved a rock under one corner of the plank. When the old man had started across, the footbridge had tipped, spilling him into the dirty water. They had been scared by their own thoughtlessness, for they certainly wouldn't have done it, had they known the old man was going to fall. They had expected him only to stagger a little as he crossed the wobbly plank. They never thought before they did something. All they thought about was having fun.

With difficulty Old Abe had clambered out of the ditch.

"Good work, boys! Good work! Well done!" a sarcastic voice had said behind them, and the dark eyes of

Pastor Larens looked at them with sharp reproof. They had blushed and run away, ashamed of themselves.

"Good work!" the preacher had said, and that had hurt. If he had boxed their ears or given them a firm scolding, it would not have hurt half as badly as those sarcastic words, "Good work! Well done!" Yes, it had hurt. They understood what the pastor meant, and were deeply ashamed of themselves.

"Good work!" Pastor Larens had spoken those words once before, when Hugh and Henry had rescued Blackie from the burning stable. At that time they had been proud of the minister's words, and he had told the farmer what they had done. Mr. Jackson had given each of them two shiny, new silver dollars to put in their piggy banks.

They watched as the pastor helped Old Abe up to the side of the ditch. For a moment the old man had gripped the pastor's hand, and then he had hurriedly plodded off in his wet clothes.

The preacher had told no one about their prank—not their parents or their teachers. This made the boys even more ashamed of themselves. They no longer dared to look the pastor in the eyes. Earlier that afternoon, when they had seen the pastor coming down the street toward them they had quickly ducked into a side street.

Now they were walking on along the narrow dike.

"I know a trick," said Henry. He lay down flat on his stomach, his arms on his back, and tried to get up without using his arms or rolling over. It wasn't easy, but he finally managed it. Jimmy tried it, and he too finally mastered the trick. But fat Hugh just couldn't do it. Laughing uproariously, he rolled over and over down the side of the dike, ending upright on the edge of the swamp.

"A boat, you guys! Old Abe's boat!" Henry said excitedly but also a bit uneasily. Jimmy just looked frightened, but Hugh, still lying on his stomach, lifted his red face in curiosity.

The boat lay nearby, tied up among the reeds at the water's edge. Henry's eyes sparkled delightedly as a plan came into his head, but something made him hesitate for a moment.

"Let's go for a boat ride! We'll just go back and forth between the reeds a little ways," he whispered, as if he were afraid to say it out loud.

Hugh was always ready for fun and adventure. It looked a bit risky, but he was more than willing. Jimmy pulled a frightened face. He brought forward a hundred reasons why they shouldn't, but in the end he went along, as usual.

For a while the boys amused themselves by rocking the boat where it was tied. Then they untied it, and slowly the vessel drifted into open water, rocking gently. This was even more fun! Old Abe? He wouldn't be looking for his boat this afternoon anyway.

"Left, Hugh! Steer to the left, or else Old Abe will see us from his cabin. He's not coming, is he?"

"Of course not!" laughed Hugh, starting to enjoy himself more and more.

Jimmy squatted down in the bottom of the boat, where he felt himself safer.

The boat bobbed gently up and down, floating farther and farther away from shore.

The boys were having tremendous fun! But they didn't stop to think. Merrily they bobbed along on dappling waves which seemed to smile happily up at them.

They didn't see the dark shadow that passed across the swamp like a sudden frown. In the distance evening mists were beginning to creep out over the water. Dark clouds were gathering on the horizon and the rustling reeds began moaning mournfully.

Abe was sitting in his cabin mending his nets. It was getting dark, and the fading light wove a halo in his white hair. He sat with his hands resting on the net in his lap, and listened. Outside the wind was picking up.

Abe sat staring out ahead of him lost in somber thought. The wind was getting stronger. Listen to it howl. A storm was brewing. Abe knew that restless sound; it would build up to a much wilder, much more violent tempo soon. But that was all right. He welcomed it.

Listen to it whistling and howling across the water! It was like the storm that was raging in Abe's heart too. The wind rushed on restlessly as if driven by fear. That was how he was driven too—on and on, with never a place to rest. Ah, listen to it howl. That was good, very good.

The wild wind, the raging storm, the threatening clouds—they were all Abe's faithful friends, just as dark, lonely and fearful as he.

It was getting darker. The old man lit his lamp.

Outside the wind came in ever stronger gusts, roaring plaintively. And Old Abe's soul roared too.

There was no rest for him, nowhere. Abe had tried to pray, he had wanted to tell God about his grief, he had wanted to forget his hate. But he *could* not. No, those boys, those boys!

They kept haunting his thoughts. He kept hearing them—their screaming and their taunting. When he tried to pray, those boys appeared before his eyes, laughing at him, so that he forgot his prayer. His folded hands would become threatening fists. No, he just couldn't forget his hate.

Abe knew how wicked he was. He knew that he had to wrench himself free from the grip of his hatred. Only then would the Lord Jesus hear him, and only then would his heart find rest. Sometimes he felt that the Lord wasn't angry with him, and that the Lord looked down on him with friendly eyes—eyes that were even more friendly than those of the pastor. Yes, sometimes it seemed that the Lord Jesus was stretching out a loving hand to help him—even more loving than the pastor's hand when he had helped Abe from that ditch. Yes, sometimes.

But Abe knew he could not come to the Lord Jesus because his hatred for the boys who had hurt him held him in its grip; it would not let go, ever!

Those boys . . . ! Ah, the storm was rising; the old cabin creaked and groaned. Those boys! He'd like to . . . !

The raging wind seemed to feed his own anger. He'd like to . . . !

Quiet! What was that? A voice?

The old man raised his head to hear better. Was it the wind, or the rain?

Shhh! There it was again. Listen. There was the howling of the wind and the splashing of the rain, but also something else besides. Listen, there it was again, very faint and frightened, like a call for help.

Abe listened more closely. He opened the back door, and the lamp flickered as the wind hit it.

Yes, there it was again.

The old man walked to the dock. The turbulent water of the swamp slammed against it. Bareheaded, he stood in the rain, his eyes peering into the darkness and his ears attuned to every sound.

Although Abe was old and his eyes and his ears were not as sharp as they once were, he knew the sounds of the swamp, and he seemed to be able to hear them better than other sounds. Now too he had heard right. Listen! That wasn't just the moaning of the wind. There was something else, too!

Listen! A voice! No, voices—frightened voices, screams!

The old man cupped his hand around his ear, and listened more intently still, his body leaning far over the water.

"Boys!" he suddenly roared. "They're boys! Those pests! I thought I heard them: they're boys! Let them drown, those pests! Let them drown! Let them drown just like my Jenny!"

He clenched his fist and shook it threateningly at the dark water. They must have taken *his* boat; he had forgotten to bring it around to the dock.

"Let them drown! Let them drown, the . . . the pests!"

And he would laugh about it! No one knew where they were, except him, and he would stand here and laugh—yes, laugh. Abe's rage mounted. The wind blew furiously and the rain stung his face. He stood there alone, the old man, raging darkly into the dark night, alone with his anger, forsaken and lost in the wild surge of water and wind and clouds.

"Let them drown! They have it coming! They deserve it for what they did to my Jenny and my daughter."

He turned and stumbled away.

Was that the sudden pressure of a hand on his shoulder, or was it a gust of wind? Was that a voice whispering to him, "No, Abe, you may not walk away! Go back!" or was it just the splashing rain? He hesitated. He knew it was wrong, but his hatred choked off all other feelings.

Again a cry sounded from the darkness—a hoarse, shrill scream of terror. No words. Just a screech of mortal terror.

Abe stopped. That sound reached deeper than his ears; it pierced his heart.

"What? What's that? That's my Jenny! That's how my Jenny screamed too!" Once again he heard the chilling cry from the swamp.

Abe turned around and hesitated again. In his heart raged a struggle between hatred and that better urge, the urge which had always lost before. Wasn't that his Jenny calling him? His poor Jenny? Wasn't it?

Abe's head spun. He couldn't think clearly. He no longer knew who was out there. Was it his Jenny, or

those boys? Or was it his daughter? All he heard was the
fear in those cries, the mortal fear. It was the same
horrible sound he had once heard in the voice of his dear
Jenny. And just as he had forgotten everything then, in
his all-consuming desire to save the girl, now, too, he
was possessed by the urge to save. He had to, even if he
didn't want to. He couldn't stand to hear that sound any
longer. He had to go!

A big splash! The water surged over the low dock. In
the dark water the old man swam hard in the direction
of the screams.

He could still do it. In his younger years he had been a
good swimmer. Now the wild water whipped and swirled
around him and burst over his head. With strong,
powerful strokes he pulled himself through the waves.
Furiously he struggled on, without thinking of his own
aging body. That was how he had rowed to save his
daughter and his little girl. That was how he slogged
ahead through the water now. He fought the water,
thrashing furiously with his arms, as if he were trying to
beat back the hatred which sought to engulf him.

Gasping, he spat out the water that splashed into his
mouth, as if he were ridding himself of the poison in his
heart. Harder and harder he struck out at the water in
order not to hear the voices which kept whispering,
"Go back, Abe! Why should you save those pests? What
about Jenny and your daughter? Have you gone mad?
Have you forgotten them?"

He was panting heavily, but he kept on going. Now he

could see his boat: two more strokes, one more . . . .

One boy was hanging in the water, clinging desperately to the wildly heaving boat. Another boy lay in the bottom of the boat, tightly clutching the bench.

Abe saw the mortal terror of the boys. His trembling hands reached out to them, compassion stirred in his heart. It was strange, it was warm, it was un-believable—compassion in Abe's heart!

He had not been able to save his Jenny and his daughter, but this time he would do it, he had to do it. First he would get the boy outside the boat and heave him back inside. Ah! His dark enemy still seemed to be trying to pull him back. But Abe would beat him off with his fists. He would, he had to save that boy. That warmth in his heart—it filled him like a miraculous strength.

Abe dove. He groped and searched around in the dark water until he found the dangling legs of the boy. He grabbed them, and with the strength of a young man, he thrust upward. With a thud the boy landed in the wildly rocking boat. Stunned with fear and cold he lay still on the bottom. It was Hugh, his chest was heaving pain-fully and his lips trembled. Beside him, still hanging onto the bench, was Jimmy.

Abe held on to the edge of the boat. He was tired and out of breath. The plunging boat kept dunking him un-der the waves. His eyes were closed, and his old body trembled with exhaustion. His fingers were slipping, but inside him, in his heart, was that strange happiness that made him forget his own danger.

Listen! What was that? Was that a groan he heard? Did it come from the boat? Or . . . ?

The old man looked up: a short distance from the boat a sickly pale head bobbed up and then soundlessly disappeared again. For a moment two pale hands reached above the water in a silent plea for help.

Abe was startled, not by that pale head, but by the hatred that was still with him whispering, "Let him drown! Don't look for him."

But now Abe knew his enemy, and now he fought back. Another boy? He would save him too. His dark enemy refused to let him go, but Abe felt himself being borne up by strong arms, and the miraculous joy in his heart seemed to lend strength to his own arms. He felt a hand like the hand of the pastor reaching out to him, but stronger and mightier.

"Oh Lord Jesus," he prayed, "help me to save this boy too!" With renewed strength, again the old man dove, and again he succeeded. The boy's head dragged through the storm-whipped water as Abe swam back to the boat. It seemed to the old man as if he were carrying his poor Jenny, and on his face was a look of peace.

He was beside the boat, and when the bow dipped down, he pushed the unconscious boy over the side. The old man himself clung to the side, tossed up and down by the waves. He was too exhausted to climb into the boat.

Abe was afraid, not for his own safety, but for the safety of the boys. If he were to let go of the boat, it would drift off and perhaps turn over. And then the boys would still drown, just like his Jenny. No, he couldn't allow that to happen.

Summoning all his strength, he started swimming again, pushing the boat ahead of him. Yes, he was doing it. In his heart was a prayer for help, a wordless prayer, a desperate plea for the strength to bring the boys to safety. But now he was sure that the Lord would help him, for the hatred, the terrible hatred that had always pulled him away from the Lord was gone. He was closer to the Lord Jesus now.

The old man struggled on. The boat slid through the reeds. On the dike bobbed the lights of several lanterns. There were people there, anxiously searching for the missing boys. Abe understood their fear, and momentarily the memory of that old pain tore at his heart. But it was only momentarily. Then he renewed his struggle. He had to get to shore; he had to save his Jenny, no, the boys. Or was it his daughter? He wasn't sure anymore. But he knew that he had to go on. A red haze gathered before his eyes, a marvelous glow. He felt as if he were drifting off in a cloud of light. But it wasn't frightening, it was blessedly peaceful.

The boat touched shore and hands grabbed it. Eager arms reached for the boys, and strong men pulled Old

Abe onto dry land.

The old man was unconscious. His eyes were closed. A foot kicked him, and someone cursed him. "He must have tried to drown them!" said one man. And another added, "He bewitched them!"

"Leave him alone! Our boys are back, and we don't know what happened," said Henry's father, pushing closer.

Just then, Jimmy's frightened little voice piped up, "We did it. It was our fault."

Later that night a dark form hurried along the narrow dike in the direction of the old man's cabin. It was Pastor Larens. He had heard what happened. Jimmy had told everything. Hugh and Henry had also regained consciousness, but they were still unable to talk.

Old Abe had been carried to his cabin, undressed, and put to bed. He was still alive. Slowly he had regained consciousness. But the tremendous strain had taken a heavy toll. Someone had gone to inform the pastor, and the old man had been left all alone.

Quietly, respectfully, the preacher entered and walked to the bed. The lamp was lit.

Abe was pale, and his eyes were closed. On a shelf near the bed lay a child's dress; it was neatly mended and freshly laundered. Beside it stood a little box on wheels.

The pastor put his hand on the old man's head, bent over him, and listened for his shallow breathing. Was he still alive?

Abe felt the touch of the pastor's hand. His eyelids fluttered and slowly he opened his eyes. He stared at the figure leaning over him, but didn't recognize him or where he was. He still heard the splashing of the waves and still saw the black shape of his boat ahead of him. A shapeless fear filled him. He had to go on, farther, still farther to the distant shore.

"Abe!" the pastor whispered softly. He saw the faraway, restless look in Abe's eyes.

Abe heard the voice and moved his lips, but no sound came. Carefully the preacher seized the old man under both arms and lifted him to a more comfortable position. Then he gently lowered the white head onto the blue pillow.

For a moment the old fear flashed through Abe. When that dark-clad man reached for him he was afraid that he would be dragged back from that beautiful strangeness that was coming for him, that he had felt coming for him when he was still struggling with the waves.

But then the old man suddenly saw two black arms again, snatching his little girl from the path of the car. Now he recognized him: it was the pastor, his friend.

It was his friend. Those arms wouldn't drag him back, they would bring that quiet blessedness which Abe didn't understand, but which made him happy.

Like a fearful child who sees his mother nearby and trustfully goes back to sleep, Abe lay back on the pillow and closed his eyes again.

The pastor waited. He looked at the old man as he lay there so peaceful and still. The cruel, hateful lines had disappeared from Abe's face. This was no longer the old, angry Abe. This was a tired, friendly old man. "Abe!" he whispered again.

The old man opened his eyes and tried to speak, but

could not. The pastor saw that his strength was gone.

"Abe," he said, "you don't have to talk. Your boys are safely home. It was good, Abe, what you did. The Lord in heaven saw it. He put compassion into your angry heart. He helped you and bore you up, Abe."

"Yes!" answered Abe's weak voice, and he nodded his head as if he were repeating it to himself. Yes, the Lord Jesus had reached out to him in the water. He had helped him. Abe was sure of that now. He had felt it when he was in the water; and it was good, so good, so very good!

"Yes!" he said once more.

"Yes, Abe, the Lord knows everything and He's not angry with you, even though you were angry at everyone and at all those boys. He knows everything."

"He knows everything!" muttered Abe, ". . . everything . . . about . . . my Jenny . . . and about the fire . . . and . . . ."

The pastor listened and took the old man's hand.

Abe mumbled on in a labored, broken voice that became inaudible at times.

It was a strange story, short and confused.

Abe talked, only vaguely aware whom he was talking to. He had to talk, even though it was hard for him and even though he hadn't talked so long in years.

He had often brooded about his grief. But now, finally, he could talk about it. Now it wasn't really grief anymore. His angry hatred was gone, and something else, something beautiful and marvelous, something Abe couldn't yet understand, had taken its place.

Although the confused story was hard to follow, the minister finally learned what had happened to make the old man so bitter. And he shared the old man's terrible pain. With deep compassion he stared at the old man. His hand squeezed Abe's fingers.

At last the old man fell silent. He was spent. His breath was labored, and his hands moved restlessly across the blankets. The pastor felt for his pulse. It was becoming weaker. He waited, sponging off the old man's face with water.

Once more Abe's strength seemed to return.

"Abe," whispered the preacher, "shall we pray, you and I, and tell the Lord everything?"

"Pray!" muttered Abe. "Yes, pray!"

Pastor Larens knelt beside the bed, putting his mouth close to the old man's ear. In a voice filled with emotion he pleaded, "Father in heaven, we thank You for helping Abe in his grief. His heart was angry, but you came and washed out all his hatred. Abe could not do that himself, he could only do it with Your help. You bore him up in the water so that he could save the boys. Oh Lord, his heart is still wicked and sinful, but You love him. You have always loved him. You want to forgive all his sins and make him happy. Now he pleads for Your grace; look down on him and deliver him from his evil. You are able to give him everlasting peace. Bear him up, Lord Jesus, bear him up into Your heavenly Father's house."

Abe listened, and that old, strange music sounded in his ears again. His hands lay folded on the covers, not clenched together, as they were when he was struggling with his hatred, when he couldn't pray.

He had been wicked and hateful and that pained him now. But the Lord Jesus loved him, had always loved him. And in fervent longing his heart cried for grace. It was a wordless prayer, for his lips could no longer speak. But his prayer rose from deep in his soul straight to his Savior, who alone could set him free.

A marvelous peace descended into Abe's heart, as if the Savior Himself had placed His hand on his head and as if He were saying the words Abe had heard on a Sunday morning long ago: "Come unto Me . . . and I shall give you rest!"

Abe no longer heard the preacher's words. His voice sounded farther and farther away. The old man was surrounded by light, brighter and brighter light.

Old Abe was dead.

The pastor looked at the old man. There was a smile on the white face. The look of pity had disappeared from the preacher's eyes. There was no need to feel pity for Old Abe now. "Lord Jesus, Your love is great; it is unending! We thank You, we thank You, Lord," the minister whispered.

In the early hours of the morning Pastor Larens walked back along the narrow dike. The storm had died down; in the distance a new day was dawning in a blaze of glorious colors.

During the night prayers had gone up in three houses in the village as three boys thanked God for their rescue and prayed for the man who had saved them. Their parents had prayed too.

Early the following morning, the pastor brought word of Abe's death. The strain of the rescue had been too much for his aging body. Many in the village hung their heads in shame because they had looked down on the old man for such a long time.

The pastor also told them the mystery of Old Abe—why he had been so angry and full of hate. And their shame increased.

The villagers buried the old man. The boys of the village joined in the funeral procession. Respectfully they stood at the graveside, their hands fumbling with their caps. They wanted to run away. They were afraid, but didn't know why. Their hearts pounded strangely within them and tears burned in their eyes.

The old man was given a respectful funeral and a small stone cross was set on his grave.

Reckless boys had made him lose his daughter. Reckless boys had caused his little girl to drown. And reckless boys had taken his life too.

Delivered from all his grief and pain by his Savior, the old man entered into the joy of his Lord.

Sometimes, on quiet evenings, three boys from the village wander along the narrow dike. There is no light in the lonely, dark cabin anymore. The dull window panes stare at them like blind, sad eyes.

When the boys see the cabin, a stillness enters their hearts. They avoid looking at each other. Is it regret? Is it remorse? Is it gratitude? Is it respect?

The rustling reeds murmur their whispering tunes as always. The swamp sings its soothing song, and the ripples spread across the water, farther and farther.